Scar Tissue
by
Patricia Hale

Copyright September 2018

All rights reserved. No part of this book shall be reproduced or transmitted in any form or by any means, electronic, mechanical, magnetic, photographic including photocopying, recording or by any information storage and retrieval system, without written permission of the publisher. No patent liability is assumed with respect to the use of the information contained herein. Although every precaution has been taken in the preparation of this book, the publisher and author assume no responsibility for errors or omissions. Neither is any liability assumed for damages resulting from the use of the information contained herein.

This is a work of fiction. Names, characters, places, and incidents either are the product of the author's imagination or are used fictitiously. Any resemblance to actual events or locales or persons, living or dead, is entirely coincidental.

ISBN: 978-1-940758-85-5 – Paperback
ISBN: 978-1-940758-83-1 – EPUB
ISBN: 978-1-940758-84-8 – Mobipocket

Cover Design: Rae Monet, Inc.

Published by:
Intrigue Publishing, LLC
11505 Cherry Tree Crossing Rd. #148
Cheltenham MD 20623-9998

For my muses,
Ezra, Cash, Hattie and Hayes

Scar Tissue

Scar Tissue

That's all history is, after all: scar tissue.

Stephen King
(Mr. Mercedes)

PROLOGUE

She stood at the edge of the roof and looked down eighteen stories to the sidewalk below. Empty. The wandering homeless had retired to alcoves and park benches coaxing weary legs to rest before the circuit began again. No dog howled, inciting a neighborhood echo over the snap of a twig or the patter of rats in the alleyway. She was surrounded by the abyssal stillness of a city asleep.

Above her, against a black velvet backdrop stars twinkled like eyes blinking back tears. She would be one of them soon. A jet crossed the moon's path and she thought about its passengers on their way to places she'd never see, adventures she'd never experience.

She'd destroyed what she'd been given, blessings others would kill for. She'd meant to raise them from their despair and had succeeded, but in so doing, lost herself. She was no one she wanted to know or be, no one worth a damn. She lifted her eyes to the stars and spread her arms like wings, her fingertips reaching…grasping…finding nothing. Her body descended into the temperate night air.

ONE

On the west side of North Yarmouth, Maine most of the homes are hidden. Nestled in wooded alcoves they're self-sufficient, isolated types, much like their owners. And though Griff and I are not reclusive, after working in the city all day, the quiet of country living had become more than just inviting. We'd decided it was a necessity. We Mainers like our privacy. Except of course when we need help, fast. But that was months down the road. Who could have predicted?

Turning into a long, narrow drive we followed our real estate agent, Peggy Lawson toward what was to be the first house Griff and I would own together. Massive elms lined both sides of the gravel path, their branches entwined overhead, creating a cathedral like entry. When we cleared the trees, the house came into view. I knew without going any further this was the one.

We approached the modest two-story farmhouse with its yellow clapboards and white trim in silence. The burgundy colored metal roof was the first detail I could check off my wish list. I'd seen enough people shoveling snow from roofs mid-February to know that wasn't a job I'd do. The metal roof assured me I'd never have to. But it was the broad farmer's porch that confirmed this place as home. It stretched end to end with three Adirondack rockers fluttering in June's almost-summer breeze. This house didn't have the split rail fence draped with red roses like the one we'd looked at in Freeport. It didn't have an attached garage, which Griff had deemed a necessity. But it had character. Intimate, enduring and unpretentious, this house was love at first sight.

We stepped out of Griff's antique Land Rover.

Peggy came up beside me. "It's a great house, Britt," she said nudging my shoulder with hers as though we had some woman-to-woman conspiracy. She should have been cozying up to Griff. The down payment was coming from his bank account, not mine.

"The owners have been meticulous about maintaining the old style but have incorporated upgrades that no one should live without. You know, the essentials, hot tub, sauna, home gym." She laughed as she led us up the front steps and onto the porch.

A shrill cry came from beyond the tree line to our right. I couldn't pin it down; pain or fear, animal or human. "What was that?" I looked at Peggy assuming as the realtor she'd have the answer.

"No idea," she said fumbling with the lock box that hung from the doorknob.

"But Siamese cats sound like that. I ought to know, I have three. Maybe your neighbors are cat people. Generally speaking though, it's dead quiet out here."

I glanced at Griff. He was shifting foot to foot unfazed by the wail, eager for Peggy to unlock the front door.

"Neighbors on both sides?" I asked.

"No, just on that side." She nodded in the direction of where the sound had come from. "The McKenzies are through the trees. Not too close, but close enough. You're not completely secluded. She must be out back in the pool. Maybe taking a swim."

"Or taking her cat for a dip," Griff said.

I rolled my eyes at him and turned back to Peggy. "How old are they?"

"I've only met them once. At a guess, I'd say she's late thirties, he's mid-forties."

I looked at Griff. "Your age. A little old for me."

"Wise ass." He tapped his foot as he watched Peggy spin the combination lock. "McKenzie sounds familiar. It's not the family that was in the news a few years ago? Kid went missing?"

Peggy wrinkled her nose. "I vaguely remember something like that, but I couldn't tell you if it's the same people, probably lots of McKenzies around. There we go." She pushed the door wide and ushered us through.

From the tiled entryway we stepped into a living room right out of Pottery Barn. Hardwood floor, adorned with a couple of Asian throw rugs, teak tables abutted a black leather couch, lamps with mica shades to emit a soothing warmth and a Buddha bust strategically placed in front of one window was aglow with late afternoon sun.

"Wow," was all that came out of my mouth. "Are they leaving the furniture?"

"Everything's negotiable," Peggy said. "You two wander around. Take your time."

"Why does McKenzie ring a bell?" I asked Griff. "Have we had a case under that name?"

Griff shook his head. "No. But if it's the same folks who were in the news there's a lot more to the story than our Realtor wants to share. Might put a damper on the sale of the house."

"What do you mean?"

"I'll tell you later."

"Will it change how I feel?"

"I don't think so."

The kitchen was a traditional farmhouse style with a built-in brick hearth and a huge farmers table that according to Peggy was staying. The countertops and the island had been upgraded to granite and the appliances carried the Viking seal.

"He's a chef," Peggy explained when she caught up with us and saw me standing in the center of the room with my mouth hanging open.

"Hope the appliances can tolerate going back to basics," I said.

In the basement, the gym included a stationary bike, stepper, elliptical, complete set of bar and dumbbells, a teakwood bar stocked with energy drinks (That would change. A margarita never hurt anyone.) and a flat screen TV.

I was beginning to feel like I was in an infomercial or one of those HGTV home makeover shows.

*Tired of working out? Step through the sliding glass doors onto the patio and toss a steak onto the built-in, gas grill. While it's cooking, jump into the hot tub or relax on patio furniture (*that put my newly purchased living room set to shame*). After dinner put your feet up and roast s'mores over the ceramic fire pit.*

We left Peggy looking longingly at the elliptical and headed upstairs.

The second floor held three bedrooms. The first one we looked at no doubt belonged to a little girl. Pink walls, white trim, ruffled bedspread and enough stuffed animals and dolls for the kid to open her own toy store.

"This'll do for Allie," Griff said.

"With a little work. Allie's fifteen, not five. But she'll love it after a few upgrades."

Allie was the reason Griff had begun house hunting. She and her mom, Griff's ex, had been pulled into one of our cases a few years ago as a serial killer's last hurrah. Finding them was still one of Griff's finer moments, but the scars had yet to heal and the ordeal left Allie with frequent nightmares and a plethora of fears. Griff believed a house would provide a more stable environment than his bachelor style apartment. So here we were.

The next bedroom would serve as a guestroom. With its view of the drive and the archway of trees, it promised our guests would be in no hurry to leave. When we stepped into the master bedroom, I knew Peggy had saved the best for last. Hardwood flooring with plush rugs framed the king size, four-poster bed that centered the room. Six, paned windows along the west wall permitted a smattering of leaf shadows across the floor while the sun's rays streamed unbroken through the string of skylights in the cathedral ceiling. The effect melted away the walls, leaving us with a sensation of standing in the trees.

I looked at Griff.

He smiled and raised his eyebrows.

The shower in the master bath was enclosed on two sides by walls of Mexican tile. The third wall was floor to ceiling glass and looked onto the private backyard. I wasn't sure how I'd feel showering with that window offering full disclosure to anyone who might be out back or in the trees. But who the hell would be standing in the woods in the middle of nowhere? I'm in good shape, but probably not worth the trip. The sauna was located in one corner of the bathroom, small but adequate, made of cedar with a horseshoe shaped bench running the perimeter of the wall and a rock hearth in the center.

As we turned to leave the bathroom the quiet was pierced by a single wail. The same sound we'd heard before. I looked at Griff. "What the hell is that?"

He shrugged. "Peggy's right. It sounds like a cat."

"How would you know? You've never owned a cat."

"Doesn't mean I've never heard one."

I pointed to the trees that shielded our house (or what we both knew would soon be our house) from the McKenzie's. "It's coming from over there."

"Lighten up Callahan. We're not on the job."

"I just want to know what it is." I followed him down the stairs and we stood in the living room again admiring the décor. I gazed out the floor to ceiling window into the woods beyond. "Bet it gets really dark out here at night," I said.

Peggy appeared in the front hallway and laughed. "If it's of any comfort, it does take a while to make the shift from city to country living. Darkness is all encompassing out here. You don't get that in Portland, not even in the middle of the night."

We followed her outside and I let my concern slip away. She was right. I was a city girl and had been knee deep in noise all my life. This would take some getting used to.

We walked the full circumference around the house ending up once again on the back deck. I started thinking maybe this was a joke. We were lookie-loos just wanting to see how the other half lived. I glanced at Griff and raised my eyebrows. He gave me his best poker face.

"Can I talk to you for a sec?"

Peggy took the hint and stepped away, peering through the sliding doors at the elliptical.

"Are you nuts? This place is right out of *Architectural Digest.* It has to be way out of our range unless there's something you haven't told me."

Griff laughed. "You know everything about me there is to know and yet you stay anyway."

"No, really," I said. "Why are we looking at this place?"

"The owners aren't selling to make money," Peggy said, overhearing or eavesdropping. (Realtors' ears are right on par with a bloodhound's nose.) "They want out and they want out as fast as possible. They're willing to take whatever they can get to make it happen."

"Why?"

"He's been offered a job in Paris and has to go now if he wants it."

"So why doesn't he go, and his wife stay behind and sell the house?"

"They want the whole thing to happen in one transaction. Sell. Move. Done with it. I get the feeling there's more going on, but I don't have the details. Maybe the marriage is on the rocks and they're trying to salvage it. I don't know. But they've listed it for less than half it's worth, so I know money's not an issue."

"Obviously," I said. "What if there's something wrong with the house?"

Peggy smiled. "Is this your first home purchase?"

I nodded. "My first, not his."

"That's what the home inspection is for. If there's anything wrong with the house it'll be uncovered." She turned to Griff. "Are you interested in putting together an offer, Mr. Cole?"

"Absolutely."

"When would you like to do that?"

"Yesterday."

"We can go back to my office and do it now if you have time."

"It's almost six-thirty," Griff said glancing at his watch. "Too late?"

"A sale's a sale," Peggy said. "I don't run on anyone's clock. I'm game if you are."

Griff gestured toward the door. "After you."

We walked back through the house and out the front door. I tried to take in every detail, so I could start imagining myself actually living here. It seemed impossible that this could be ours. You know that saying…if it seems too good to be true?

Outside, we waited for Peggy to lock up. Griff and I wandered around the front yard and then out to the back once again imagining our next barbeque.

"It's really quiet." I said.

He wrapped his arm around my shoulders and pulled me against him. "You'll get used to it and then I'll have to drag you into the city kicking and screaming."

I laughed. "You're probably right." I followed him along the side of the house and back toward the driveway. An unmistakable whine came from the trees. We both stopped.

"Jon, Jon…baby Jon…" The sing-song tune was barely audible.

"Did you hear a voice?" I asked Griff.

"A voice? No. Wind in the trees, maybe. The silence making you jumpy, Callahan?"

"I heard someone singing or calling for Jon."

Griff stopped and looked at me like I'd said there were cows flying overhead.

"What? Why are you looking at me like that?"

He shook his head. "Nothing. It's nothing. Let's go. Maybe the cat escaped."

"Can you be serious for a minute?"

"I am being serious. I want to get out of here and write up an offer on this place. It's not going to last long and according to Peggy we're the first ones to look at it."

"Ready?" Peggy poked her head around the corner of the porch.

"You bet," Griff said picking up his pace.

I glanced over my shoulder in the direction that the voice had come from. There was nothing, no sound. Cat, my ass. I turned and followed Griff toward the front of the house. "I'm a dog person," I said, in case anyone was listening.

TWO

Even after three months, our new Cole and Callahan P.I. Inc. sign still made me smile each time I passed beneath it. I'd begged Griff to change it from the original Cole& Co. to reflect both of us as equal partners and he'd made the upgrade after our last case. He said I'd earned it, and then some. I didn't argue.

"Where's your other half?"

I juggled my messenger bag onto my shoulder, then carefully switched my Starbucks tumbler to one hand, my brown bag lunch to the other and turned to see our office receptionist extraordinaire, Katie Nightingale, coming toward me up the sidewalk.

"Don't move a muscle," she said waving her set of office keys in the air. "I've got you covered."

"Thank God somebody does," I said with a laugh.

"Where's Griff?"

"He picked up Allie for breakfast this morning."

"And you're not joining them?"

"I think we found a house," I told her. "I wanted him to tell her the news without me in case she has any misgivings. She can vent if she needs to."

"Are you kidding? That girl loves you."

"I know, but I like to make sure she has time with her dad, without me. I don't ever want our relationship to feel competitive."

Katie pushed open the front door and I followed her up the stairway that led to our office. The messenger bag swung against my thigh half empty. We were between cases at the moment.

The light was blinking on the answering machine on Katie's desk and I stepped past her as she flopped into her swivel chair and reached for the phone to check messages. Griff and I each have our own office off the main reception area. We've found that clients are often gender specific. A woman whose husband is cheating feels less judged when she's sharing the details with another woman. Men, on the other hand want revenge and look for strength and that sways them toward Griff. We work together on every case, but the initial conversation often takes place behind the door of the client's choosing.

Katie appeared in my doorway as I took the last bite of my glazed, raspberry scone. I held up my finger asking her to wait a second. (Anything glazed takes priority.) I closed my eyes and swallowed, savoring the remnants of the most delicious and unhealthy breakfast I'd had in a long time. "Okay, what's up?" I asked once the last of the crumbs had cleared my throat.

"Message on the machine. Sounds like a new case. Parents want to discuss the death of their child that was, they believe, wrongly labeled a suicide."

"They leave a name?"

Katie nodded. "Lambert."

"As in Ashley Lambert?"

She nodded.

"Shit."

"That's what I said. To the machine, not the client."

"I remember reading about that. When was it?"

"A month ago? Maybe a little more."

I slipped a Backwoods Honey Berry from the pack in my bag and opened the window in the corner of my office. My addiction to the little cigars was Griff's pet peeve. I kept the window screen-less for just this purpose. Scooting through the frame I sat on the grated floor of the fire escape, my legs dangling inside the office and lit up.

"Google her," I said to Katie motioning to the laptop on my desk. "See what you can find."

"This is dated May 20th," Katie said. "Headline reads, Fensworth Student Jumps to Her Death. My God, look at her. She's beautiful. What a waste."

I leaned inside and looked at a face right off a Cover Girl advertisement. Flawless skin and sculptured cheekbones gave way to a broad smile and straight white teeth. A blond ponytail all but swayed from the back of her head and feathered bangs accented huge blue eyes. Lithe and athletic, Ashley stood beside a hurdle on a Tartan track, a two-foot trophy in her hand.

"Are you saying if she was a four instead of a ten it would be less tragic?"

"Sounded that way, didn't it?" Katie said. "I didn't know I was that shallow."

I nodded toward the computer. "Keep reading."

"Twenty-one-year-old Ashley Lambert jumped to her death from the rooftop of the eighteen-story Bayside building. The high rise is located on the corner of Front St. and Canterbury Ave. in downtown Portland. Jesus," Katie interjected shaking her head. "Ms. Lambert was a senior at the elite Fensworth College in southern Maine. She'd just completed an undergraduate degree in Behavioral Science with a minor in Philosophy and had been accepted to the prestigious Johns Hopkins Berman Institute, in pursuit of a masters degree in Bioethics. Along with her excellence in academics, Ms. Lambert was named Woman Outdoor Track Athlete of the Year for the third straight year. The Lambert family is requesting privacy at this time and asking that donations be made in Ashley's name to the Berman Institute."

"May 20th, that's roughly a week before graduation, why would a student, especially a student with this bright a future, kill herself? It doesn't make sense. Look at her accomplishments."

"I can't," Katie said. "It makes me want to kill myself."

I shook my head. "Stop. This is tragic."

"I know," she said. "And from the message on the machine I'd say her parents feel the same way. They don't get it."

The office's outer door opened and a moment later Griff appeared in my doorway. "Sneaking a quick one?" he asked.

I stubbed out what was left of my cigar on the fire escape leaving a gray smudge on the black iron grate and slid inside.

"We got a call."

He raised his eyebrows.

"Ashley Lambert's parents."

"The jumper?"

I nodded.

"What do they need us for?"

"They just left a message. Sounds like they're either unhappy with the ME's assessment of suicide or they accept it and want to know why." I followed him into his office. "How's Allie?"

"She's great. I told her about the house. She can't wait to see it. Hopefully we'll hear something today regarding the offer and I'll take her out there tonight to look at it."

Katie stepped into the office with a mug of coffee for Griff and the Lamberts' phone number. "Here you go," she said. "They didn't leave any information except their phone and a request for a call back."

"Thanks," Griff said raising the mug and taking a sip. "If a Peggy Lawson calls, interrupt me."

"Will do," she said and pulled the door closed behind her.

I sank into the buttery brown leather armchair beside my desk. "Hey, we got so caught up in putting together the offer last night that I completely forgot to ask you what you meant when you said Peggy was leaving something out about the McKenzies."

"Oh yeah, I forgot too." He settled into his desk chair and leaned forward with both hands wrapped around his coffee mug.

Story time.

"You must remember. It was about four years ago, and it was all over the news."

"Four years ago, I'd just left the law practice. I was not at my best."

"Oh, right, but still, it was a major story. McKenzie's kid went missing. Around a year old, I think. The kid just vanished."

"Oh shit, yeah. Now I remember, vaguely."

"They never figured out what happened to him."

"Him? A little boy?"

Griff nodded. "Jonathan as I remember."

I looked at him. "Seriously? Jonathan?"

"Mmm."

"That's why you freaked out when I said I heard someone call for Jon last night."

"Mmm."

"So, it is the same family?"

"Mmm."

"Griff, say something more than 'mmm,' will you?"

"What'd you want me to say?"

"Tell me about it. I don't remember the details."

"The case stretched on forever. McKenzie is a Portland cop, so obviously the investigation was a large-scale operation, top priority, feds, search dogs, the whole nine yards. They interviewed and re-interviewed everyone within a hundred miles."

"A hundred miles?"

"Okay, I'm exaggerating, but the point is they went above and beyond, meticulous scrutiny of every detail, neighbor, babysitter, delivery people, anyone and everyone the parents had even the slightest affiliation with. They put both parents and every relative through hell. Interrogated them for hours and in some cases, days. In the end, they found absolutely nothing. The kid vanished. You remember any of this?"

"Yeah, I do now, pretty creepy."

"Ah uh."

"So why do you think Peggy held that back?"

"You said it yourself. It's creepy. No real estate agent wants to volunteer creepy neighbor stuff when they're trying to sell a house."

"Thought they were obligated to disclose information?"

"About the house, not about the neighbors."

I thought for a minute. "The fact that the neighbors lost their kid doesn't change my mind about wanting the house. Is that cold?"

"If you're cold, I'm frigid 'cause nothing is going to stop me from getting that place for us."

I walked around the desk, wrapped my arms around his shoulders and nuzzled into his neck. "There's nothing frigid about you, baby."

"I'm imagining us slipping into the hot tub after a dip in the pool."

"There's no pool."

"There will be. We just need a couple of cases to cover it."

"Speaking of which." I stretched one arm onto my desk and picked up the Lambert's phone number that Katie had left.

He kissed my hand and slipped the paper from my fingers. "Time to get to work."

THREE

The Lamberts' address was in Cape Elizabeth, a twelve-mile peninsula stretching into open-ocean and marking the entrance of Casco Bay. It's one of southern Maine's most prestigious towns, ranking in wealth alongside Ogunquit and Kennebunkport (think Bush compound). It's also the lucky guardian of Fort Williams, a recreational park along the southern seacoast. A sub-post during World War II, the park has now become a favorite of dog walkers, kite fliers and family outings. The crumbling rock lookout stations once used to protect the harbor have been turned over to the imaginations of visiting children. Ducking in and out of darkened tunnels, they crouch in the bird's nest, no longer fighting off enemy ships, but each other, with plastic ray guns instead of M1 Carbines. (Progress? You decide.) Fort Williams is also home to the Portland Headlight, one of the most photographed lighthouses in the world and at the top of the list along with Acadia National Park as places to visit in Maine.

Griff slowed and turned right onto Cousins Ave. We watched mailboxes until we came to #57. He pulled tight to the curb and cut the engine. The house was modest compared to many of its neighbors, but the ocean view I glimpsed through the trees put it easily in the million-dollar range and then some. I think the style is called English Tudor, a combination of stonework and decorative timber with gables and parapets that had me wavering between impressed and leery. It might be inviting when sunlight warmed the iron-grated windows, but under today's gunmetal sky it stood dark and ominous.

"You told them we were coming, right?" I asked as we got out of the car.

"Yeah, Mr. Lambert said one o'clock." Griff glanced at his watch. "We're right on time. Why?"

"No lights."

"Not everyone's afraid of the dark, Callahan."

I planted a soft right against his shoulder. He caught it and gave it a twist, spinning me into him. "I missed you at breakfast this morning," he said.

"I wanted you to have time alone with Allie. Anyway, when we move into the house we'll have breakfast together every day."

"Can't happen soon enough." He snuck a kiss and we sauntered up the Lamberts' driveway side by side.

Griff had been talking about living together for over a year and brought up the M word with some frequency. The closest I've been able to get is to agree to share a house with him. Though he's never met my parents (and never will) he's heard enough about my childhood to understand why I shy away. It's my good fortune that he's a patient man.

The door opened before we'd made it onto the threshold, indicating Mr. Lambert had been waiting for us. I imagined him peering out from behind the darkened windows, his eyes roaming up and down the street, watching.

"Mr. Lambert?" Griff stepped onto the cement step at the door and extended his hand. "I'm Griff Cole."

The men shook and then Griff turned to me. "My partner, Britt Callahan."

I started to reach for Mr. Lambert's hand but let mine fall back to my side when he didn't offer his own. He simply nodded in my direction, turned and led us inside. (Strike one.)

We followed him across a tiled entry, a massive chandelier hung overhead. The house was dark inside despite its many windows. Heavy velvet drapes didn't give daylight a chance. A banister of deep cherry corralled a wide staircase to our right and stretched the full length of the second-floor hallway above. Greg Lambert stopped in front of a set of French doors and in one motion opened both towards us. We stepped onto a brick patio. Despite the gray day the landscaped garden in front of us was breathtaking and must be spectacular in sunshine. A woman knelt beside one of the many wood-enclosed, raised flowerbeds. Her face hid beneath a wide brimmed straw hat while her gloved hands trimmed back leaves with an artist's touch. The contrast between the home's somber interior and this outdoor garden was like stepping through a time warp.

"They're here," Mr. Lambert said.

Without looking up, the woman rose to her feet. She walked toward us, her arm outstretched. This time I was on the receiving end.

"I'm Britt," I said taking her hand in both of mine.

She was extremely thin, almost waiflike. Strands of blond hair had slipped from the bun beneath her hat and framed a face that had not only been sheltered from the sun, but from the harsher things in life. It was a face accustomed to money and what it provided. But as much as her flawless skin radiated wealth, her eyes radiated pain. I wondered if her grief commenced with the death of her daughter or if it went part and parcel with a husband who so far, seemed as devoid of warmth as the house they lived in.

"I know who you are," she said. "I do my research."

Not sure how to respond to that, I turned to Griff. He was looking from one Lambert to the other fighting off a grin. He has a tendency to be amused by weirdoes, while I get plain annoyed.

A woman in black yoga pants and a striped tee shirt stepped out of the house and approached us with lithe grace. "Can I bring you some coffee? Iced tea, perhaps?" she asked.

The resemblance between the two women was unmistakable, but their demeanors were polar opposites. This woman floated while Mrs. Lambert's every movement was weighted and slow, to the point of looking painful.

"I'll have tea," I told her.

"Coffee for the rest of us," Mr. Lambert said.

"Thank you, Carole," Mrs. Lambert's voice was little more than a whisper. The woman disappeared inside the house. "Carole's my sister. She's been coming over to help me since, since…" she let the rest of the sentence drop.

"Have a seat." Mr. Lambert gestured us toward a group of cushioned rattan chairs perfectly arranged around a circular marble table.

"Call me Greg," he said as we sat. "My wife is Guinevere."

I nodded toward Guinevere hoping to catch her eye, but she didn't look up. She was studying the flower she held in her hand, a columbine. A flower frequently linked to birds. Its name is derived from the Latin word columba, a reference to doves.

(Sometimes I surprise myself with the tidbits of wisdom lodged in my brain. The species connection to the afterlife didn't escape me either.)

"Is Carole your only sibling?" I asked hoping to draw Guinevere out with a little small talk to start.

She raised her eyes, appraising me like a new piece of jewelry. "I have a step-brother. We're estranged."

So much for chitchat. "I'm sorry."

"Don't be. There's no animosity. He lived with his mother. Paternal genes are all we have in common."

Carole returned and set a small round tray of coffee, tea and cookies in the middle of the table. Greg watched her, tilting his head to one side and folding his arms across his chest. Annoyed, his body said. When she'd finished, he spoke.

"I don't believe my daughter jumped. She wouldn't have done that. I told the police, but they dismissed me. Evidently, they knew my daughter better than I did."

"What's your feeling on that, Mrs. Lambert?" I asked. Parents don't always share perspectives on their children.

When she looked at me, her eyes were moist. She cradled the columbine in her palm. "Call me Gwen."

I nodded.

"Ashley was a good girl. She worked very hard at everything she did."

"She was the best, always. She made sure of it," Greg chimed in.

Or else you did, I thought.

"It would have gone against her nature to jump off that building. It just wasn't her way," Gwen added.

"Her way?" Greg squinted at his wife, his face twisted in disgust as though studying an insect on flypaper. "What the hell does that mean?" He stood and walked around the circumference of our seating arrangement and then came back and took his chair again. "My girl did as she was told. And only what she was told."

"It's not always easy to tell a senior in college what to do," I said. "At some point, they start making their own choices even if some are ones their parents might not like."

"Not my girl." Greg shook his head.

I couldn't help but notice he kept referring to Ashley as *my* girl not our girl as though he'd created her, given birth and raised her singlehandedly. I didn't like him. My assessment of Gwen was still up in the air, but she was wrapped so tight I couldn't get a glimpse inside.

"She was a star athlete at the top of her class and a week from graduation," Greg continued. "She'd been accepted at Johns Hopkins Berman Institute for Bioethics. And you're telling me that's a kid who makes bad decisions? I don't think so, Ms. Callahan."

"Mr. Lambert - Greg," Griff spoke up. "I have a daughter. I can't imagine what you must be going through dealing with all this. What is it you think we can do for you?"

"I told the police and the medical examiner that my daughter wouldn't take her own life. Cops shook their heads, said it wasn't their call to make. The medical examiner said it presented as a cut and dried suicide."

"And what do you say, Mr. Lambert?"

"My daughter was murdered."

I glanced at Gwen. "Do you agree, Mrs. Lambert?"

She raised her eyes, glanced at her husband and then to me. "I'm not convinced, but I do agree that suicide doesn't fit with who my daughter was."

Griff kept his focus on Greg. "What makes you think someone would have killed your daughter? Did she have enemies that you're aware of?"

"No, no enemies that I know of, but her jumping makes no sense. She had everything going for her and absolutely no reason to end her life. She would never have done that to me."

Strike two. The selfish bastard assumed his daughter's tragic death had more to do with him than whatever had driven her to that fateful state of mind. "Suicide is about what's going on within the person themselves," I said trying not to let my voice betray my disgust. "I doubt Ashley was consciously doing anything to you at the moment she jumped. If she jumped."

"She knew the goals we'd set," he said dismissing my remark. "And she had every intention of attaining them."

"Goals?" I asked.

"Johns Hopkins, her PhD, an Olympic gold medal."

"Had she been accepted to compete in the Olympics?" Griff asked.

"It was in the works," he said annunciating each word as though we were hard of hearing.

"Did you let the medical examiner know how you felt?"

"Of course, I did."

"And was an autopsy performed?"

Greg Lambert glanced at his wife. She looked away. Touchy subject, I gathered.

"Useless," he said. "They found nothing." He turned to Gwen. "Go get my checkbook."

She rose and disappeared inside the house without a word, still holding the columbine in her hand.

I caught Griff's eye and he raised his eyebrows as though asking, *should we?* "Look Mr. Lambert," he said. "Britt and I like to discuss a case before we commit to it. We want to feel some degree of surety that we can help you before money changes hands and we sign a contract. Give us time to talk it over and we'll get back to you tomorrow."

Gwen reappeared holding a large, black-spiraled checkbook. Greg took it from her along with the pen she offered and flipped open the front of the book. He looked at Griff. "How much do you want?" he asked.

"Mr. Lambert, I…" Griff started.

"We'll give you the information you need to get started. I don't have any doubt you'll see it my way. What's the retainer?" He held the pen poised over the checkbook.

"Five thousand," Griff said.

I thought that was a little high. He must be thinking about the pool.

"And a list of names. Professors, coaches and friends," he added.

Greg pointed to his wife. "Put that together."

Dismissed, Gwen went inside to gather what we needed.

Once we had the necessary information from Gwen, and Greg's check was folded inside Griff's pocket, Carole stepped onto the patio and offered to show us out.

"We'll be in touch," Griff said. He stood extending a hand toward Greg.

Greg Lambert rose from his chair and placed his hands on his hips. "When?"

"As soon as I have something to tell you," Griff said lowering his arm.

Griff's ability to come off unfazed by blatant rude behavior is beyond me. I couldn't get off that porch fast enough. If I'd lingered I would have placed a well-directed snap kick to Greg Lambert's groin.

We followed Carole to the front door. She swung it wide and stepped with us outside then pulled the door closed behind her. On the front step, she glanced from one of us to the other then dropped her head and stared at the granite, clearly trying to make up her mind. We waited. When she looked up she extended her arm toward Griff as though intending to shake.

"Look," she said. "I'm probably way out of line here and dipshit in there will have me banned if he knows I'm talking to you. I'm already on probation around here so whatever I say stays between us, alright?"

Griff nodded and reached for her hand, keeping his eyes on her face.

She slipped a folded piece of paper into his palm. "Call me," she said. "There's more to this. A lot more."

FOUR

"What do you think?" Griff asked once we were inside his car with the doors closed.

"The case is interesting, but Greg Lambert sucks."

"Agreed. Are we taking it?"

"His check is in your pocket."

"Easy enough to tear up."

"I'm on the fence but leaning toward taking it. As put off as I am by Greg, he's right. Ashley's suicide makes no sense. And Carole lured me in with the carrot she just dangled in front of us." I slipped a Honey Berry from the pack in my purse.

"Not in my car," Griff said reaching for the cigar.

"I'm not lighting it. I know the rules."

"It's nice to have power."

"Maybe you and Greg Lambert can be friends."

He glanced at me from the corner of his eye and frowned. "You agree with Lambert that she didn't jump?" He tipped his blinker and took a left.

"If she didn't jump then we're looking at a homicide. I'm not ready to make that leap. No pun intended. But saying she was pushed doesn't have to mean physically. Greg Lambert's a control freak. Maybe Ashley was too. Or maybe she developed buyers' remorse."

Griff flipped the visor down as the sun made its debut into the afternoon.

"What do you mean by that?"

"Fear of success."

"But she'd made it happen."

"Yeah, but sometimes people push for something and then when they get it they panic. Like, oh shit, now what do I do? You see it in musicians all the time or actors. They hit it big and the next thing you know they're in rehab 'cause once they finally make it they can't cope with their success."

Griff looked at me and raised his eyebrows. "I guess that's what we have to find out."

I squirmed sideways beneath my seat belt and looked at him. "So, you believe she jumped?"

He nodded. "I think she did. We just have to find out who pushed her."

Before I could tell him that didn't make sense his cell phone rang, and he put me on hold.

"After a brief series of okays and uh huh, he hung up. That was Peggy." He picked up my hand, raised it to his mouth and kissed my fingers. "They accepted our offer. We're home owners...almost."

I clicked off my seat belt and leaned across the seat nuzzling his neck while my heart skipped into overdrive. With the exception of my parents and college roommate, I'd never lived with anyone. This would take me that much closer to the M word. But the truth is, since our last case I'd been more receptive to the idea. What if no one had come looking for me? I might still be in that bar in Canada trading sex for food. I'd found the girl we'd been searching for by maintaining my cover as one of "the girls". Griff is adamant that my actions took guts and saved my life. But my memories are nothing like the picture he paints. To me, I'm tainted goods. To him, I'm a hero. Who wouldn't marry the guy?

"You okay?" he asked.

I nodded and slipped back into my seat. "That's great news," I said, hoping my voice was steady enough to convince us both.

"It'll be good, you'll see." His hand dropped to my leg. "And if it's not, I won't stop you from leaving."

Whenever he says shit like that...giving me an out, I know I'll never leave him. It's his strategy and it works. He knows my fear of marriage is related to the home I grew up in. And though he doesn't sleep around and I'm not a narcissistic drunk, my scars still run deep. He respects that and always offers me a way out. The thing is, I know I'll never take it. I think he does too.

"Peggy will set up a home inspection and let us know within the next day or two. We need to have the bank send out an appraiser and I've got to get Allie over there to look at it. Not that I need her approval, but you know."

"Yeah." I laughed. "You need her approval."

It was good to see Griff happy instead of weighted down by the guilt he carries around. When a case goes bad he tends to file it under personal failure. I wouldn't change who he is for anything, but I would erase a few of the worry lines that wrinkle his forehead, at least the ones I've put there.

"Peggy said she was headed to the house in about an hour to change the sign out front to Under Contract. What do you say we pick up Allie and meet her out there?"

"What do you want to do about Carole?"

"Set up a meeting for tomorrow morning. I'll call Allie and tell her we're on our way." He turned the car in the direction of Eliza's house half mumbling, half humming John Mellencamp's *Small Town* and tapping out the beat on the steering wheel.

Yeah, I'm definitely in the right place.

"What do you think?" Griff asked after giving Allie a tour of the house.

"Awesome. I love it. How soon are you moving in?"

"As soon as we close on it." Griff looked at Peggy. "And that takes?"

"Forty-five days is standard, but we can often cut it to about thirty."

"Thirty days? Why so long?" Allie asked.

"Paperwork," Griff said wrapping his palm around the back of Allie's neck and giving her a squeeze. "C'mon, let's take a walk outside."

I followed them across the kitchen and through the French doors that opened onto the middle level of the deck, above the weight room and below the master bedroom balcony. Beyond the trees I could see the dark roof of the McKenzie's and beneath it, the second story of their white colonial. We took the stairs to the lower platform and stood beside the sliding glass doors of the exercise room.

"This place is amazing," Allie said peering through the glass, her hands cupped around her eyes.

"The door is open," Peggy said. "Go on in."

Allie slid the glass along its runner and went for the elliptical. Stepping on, she set it in motion. "Can we keep this?"

Griff looked at Peggy.

"I told the owners you'd make a list of what you'd like them to leave with the house. They're very open to the idea. As I said they're heading for Europe. They don't want to deal with furniture. Replacing their belongings will be a lot easier than shipping them."

"They can leave everything as far as I'm concerned," Griff said. "What we don't want we'll get rid of."

"Wait a minute," I said coming up beside him. "You mean we don't have room for my IKEA kitchen set?"

"You're going to have to learn to live with the farmer's table instead," Griff said with a laugh.

"Consider it done."

"Can you tear yourself off that thing?" Griff called to Allie who was inside huffing and puffing.

"Only because I know it will be here when I come back." She stepped off the machine and came through the slider toward us.

Peggy took the keys from her pocket and went to lock the house up while Allie and Griff and I wandered toward the front yard. We'd just reached Griff's Land Rover when a man and a woman stepped out of the trees. The man was dressed in cycling shorts and a neon green, nylon shirt. The woman with him looked miserable in a blue, sleeveless maternity dress. He smiled and extended his hand. "You our new neighbors?"

Griff moved toward them and took the guy's hand. "We will be as soon as the paperwork's done."

"Welcome to the neighborhood, if you want to call it that. Not exactly your typical suburb. I'm Mike McKenzie."

"Griff Cole, and this is just the way we like it," he waved a hand toward the tree line. "We get plenty of noise in the city all day."

"I hear ya. I work with the Portland PD. It's nice to come home to peace and quiet."

"We're looking forward to it." Griff said. "This is my girlfriend, partner, and soon to be housemate, Britt Callahan."

"Housemate." I laughed and stepped forward to shake Mike's hand.

"And my daughter, Allie," Griff added. "Also, to be my housemate, at least part time."

"Hi," Allie said with a wave of her hand. She nodded to Mike's attire. "You heading out for a ride?"

"Just got back. There're some great back roads out here for biking. You ride?"

"I'm hoping for a new bike for my birthday." She glanced at Griff. "I want to get into it."

"Good for you. Let me know when you get one. I'll show you some routes. Oh," he said almost as an afterthought, this is my wife, Rhea." He reached behind him and wrapped his hand around the woman's bicep, moving her forward.

"Nice to meet you, Rhea." And then acknowledging the bulge at her midsection, I added, "When are you due?"

"Two months," she said.

Rather than the usual heightened animation of an expectant mother, her leaden voice held no trace of joy and our conversation skipped a beat.

"Well congratulations," I said breaking the momentary silence. "That's exciting. I think we heard you out here the other day when we first looked at the house. There were sounds coming from the trees."

Mike gave her a sharp look. So quick you had to be paying attention, but I was.

"Oh," he laughed. "You might have. Pregnancy makes her restless. She takes a walk sometimes through the path." He nodded behind him. "I tell her to stay in the yard. Too many roots to trip on." He put a hand on her belly. "That's the last thing we need right now."

Rhea kept her eyes on the ground and seemed unaware of our conversation.

"Right honey?" Mike asked nudging her from her world.

"For the first time, she looked up and her eyes fell on Allie. "You have beautiful hair," she said.

"Oh my God." Allie's hand shot to the tangled pile of curls wrapped in a scrunchy on top of her head. "I didn't even wash it today. But thank you."

"I used to be a hairdresser." Rhea touched her amber coif, much in need of a brush. "I'll do it for you sometime if you like."

Allie giggled. "Cool." The standard response of an uncomfortable fifteen-year- old.

"Well, we should let you go. Just wanted to say hello," Mike said. With his hand still gripping his wife's bicep, he steered her away from us and back into the trees. "We'll get together once you move in," he called over his shoulder.

"Sounds good," Griff answered with a wave and we turned back toward the car where Peggy stood waiting.

"I see you met the McKenzies," she said. "He's very nice. She's a little off, I think. Can't blame her I suppose given what she's been through. You were right," she said turning to Griff. "They are the McKenzies who lost their son."

Griff looked at me and rolled his eyes, like she hadn't known that the first time the question came up. She wanted to wait until we'd signed the offer before confirming that a crime had taken place next door or at least the possibility of a crime.

"What's that?" I asked playing dumb. I wanted to hear Peggy's rendition of the story.

"You didn't hear about it? I'm surprised. It was publicized about as much as the Lindbergh baby. Four years ago, their one-year-old son went missing. No trace of him, he just disappeared."

"They never found him?" I asked.

Peggy shook her head. "Nothing. The police scoured that house, called in the FBI, but no one ever found a trace of a lead. No foul play. They interrogated Rhea and Mike for hours, for days, really. Every delivery person, utility people, no rock left unturned as they say, and they still came up with nothing. She was home at the time and told police that little Jonathan was playing in the living room while she made lunch. When she checked on him, he was gone."

"That's horrible," I said as we walked toward our cars. "How do you cope with losing a child like that? The never knowing would drive me crazy."

Peggy nodded. "I hope she's up to caring for another one."

"Maybe that'll be the best thing for her," Griff said.

"You'd like to think so." Peggy dropped the house key in her bag. "I'll call you when I have the inspection set up."

"Hungry?" Griff asked us as we followed Peggy onto the main road and turned toward Portland.

"Starving, but I promised I'd come right home after seeing the house. The nurse leaves at 4 o'clock and Mom's still terrified of being alone."

Griff let out a long sigh and pursed his lips. I wasn't sure if he was angry over the constraints Eliza put on Allie or over the whole ordeal that had left his daughter and his ex so fragile.

"Okay, kiddo, "Home sweet home."

We took the entry ramp onto Route 295 south. From the weight of Griff's foot on the gas pedal, I knew his anger hadn't dissipated. Not until we'd passed through the gated entry at Elmwood Estates did I feel his tension dissolve. He'd accepted the need to return Allie to her mother, regardless of the reason.

Elmwood estates had become home a year ago. Eliza still owned the lakefront bungalow that she and Griff had purchased as a fixer-upper early in their marriage. But that was a rental property now. The condominium complex was closer to Allie's school and easier for Eliza to maintain in her current state.

"Pretty soon I'll have two home sweet homes," Allie said stepping out of the car. "Thanks Dad, I love the house and I know part of the reason you're doing this is for me and I'm grateful. I mean, just think of the parties I can have once the pool goes in." She flashed him a gotcha grin and closed the car door.

"You might have just given me reason to rethink this whole thing," Griff called to her out the window.

She trotted up the driveway on coltish legs, her height a gift from Griff. At the door, she looked back at him laughing and with a wave disappeared inside.

"Can't imagine what the Lamberts are going through," Griff said, his eyes still resting on the house. "But I feel like I came close."

"The difference is, Ashley Lambert was in the driver's seat of her own situation."

"She might have been sitting in the driver's seat, but I'm not convinced she was at the controls," Griff said as he backed the car onto the road.

FIVE

The next morning instead of heading for the office, we kept our appointment with Carole Weston. She'd asked us to meet her at Denny's in South Portland. Not my choice for a healthy breakfast, unless you consider white flour and sugar a good way to start the day. (Muffins being the exception. And anything with icing.)

She redeemed herself when we parked beside her in the lot. Stepping from her red BMW, she raised a hand toward the restaurant. "Sorry for this, but I needed to be sure no one I know would see me talking with you. I'm not a frequent flier."

"You mean you've never indulged in Moons Over My Hammy at two in the morning?" Griff asked.

Carole laughed. "Is that a real thing?"

"Check the menu," he said and pulled the door open, stepping aside for Carole and me to pass.

"And you know this how?" I looked at him as I entered the restaurant.

"Only once." He held his hands up in surrender. "But I savored every cholesterol laden bite."

"It's been five years and I'm still learning things about you."

"I guess that keeps me interesting."

"Depends on the topic. Moons Over My Hammy? Not so much."

The hostess seated us at a corner table in the back of the restaurant as though she knew we were flying under the radar. After delivering coffee all around and taking our breakfast order, the waitress pushed through a set of swinging doors that led to the kitchen. Only then did Carole begin talking.

"What's your opinion so far?" she asked, her eyes flipping from me to Griff.

"He's a dick," I volunteered. "As far as Gwen goes, she didn't say enough for me to form an opinion. And Ashley? The perfect child, which is the only place I'm in agreement with Greg. Her suicide doesn't make sense."

Carole glanced at Griff and raised her eyebrows.

"Greg's manning the controls, over his wife at least and if it's that way with her, I could assume it was that way with Ashley. Maybe she hit a breaking point."

Carole nodded. "He handles Gwen, always has, but Ashley was a bit of a different story."

"How so?" Griff asked.

"They were never close until recently. Clayton was Gregg's whole world."

"Clayton?"

"Their son. He was fifteen-years-old when he died. Hodgkin's Lymphoma. Ashley was at the end of her junior year in high school."

"They didn't mention him."

"No, I'm sure they didn't. But he's front and center in Ashley's striving for perfection."

"Isn't Hodgkin's rare at that age?" I asked.

"It is. Only about ten to fifteen percent of cases hit children and teens. When he was diagnosed it was like the ground opened and swallowed them all. But Greg…after Clayton died Greg became almost non-existent within the household. For him, the sun rose and set on Clayton and when he was gone it was like he'd taken Greg with him. Ashley had always been more of an afterthought to her father. It wasn't until she took off in track, literally, that he began taking an interest in her."

"And Gwen? How did she handle Clayton's death?"

She fell apart of course. I guess that's to be expected. What mother wouldn't? She sold the nursery she'd run for fifteen years. It was her home away from home. The kids grew up there, went to work with her every day until they reached school age. I don't think she realized it at the time, but giving up the nursery was probably the worst thing she could have done. It became another loss to grieve."

"How was their marriage after losing Clayton?" Griff asked. "I mean, they're together, but are they really together?"

"Greg has always been an ass. He and I never hit it off, even before they were married, but he's a provider. I'm sure you noticed when you were at the house. Gwen doesn't want for anything. I've never been sure if she married him out of love or need."

"If she had her own nursery she must have done all right financially," I said. "She could have left him."

"I don't mean financial need. I don't think the money means much to her.

Gwen has always needed a man to control her life. Growing up it was our dad. He controlled everything we did and not in a good way."

"He was physical?"

Carole nodded. "He knocked my mother around. He didn't touch us kids, but it was a rare day my mom escaped a back hand if his coffee wasn't hot enough."

"Is that why his first marriage failed?"

"First marriage?"

"Gwen mentioned that you have a step-brother."

"Oh yeah, Michael. No, he was the product of an affair. I never knew him well. Neither did Gwen even though his mother tried her best to inject him into our family. She actually dropped him off one day while Gwen was having an end-of-the- school-year pool party."

"Didn't go well?" I asked.

"That's an understatement. Let's just say Gwen wasn't the kindest teenager. She proceeded to point out to the laughter of her elite, cheerleader friends everything her stepbrother lacked, starting with his financials and ending with his physique. He left in a hurry."

"Can't say I blame him," Griff sympathized.

"Yeah, and that wasn't the only time she did it. The three of us were close in age, so we ran into each other often enough at the movie theater or a party even though we were at different schools. Small town, you know?"

"Michael's mother was a chambermaid at the Best Western. There was a lot of animosity between her and my dad. Gwen and I were in private school and she needed food stamps to feed Michael. I think when she got pregnant she was hoping her child would get a taste of the good life. But it didn't happen."

"She didn't get child support?"

"From what I've gathered, it was sporadic at best. My mother fought like hell not to give 'that woman and her brat', as she called them, a dime."

"Didn't the state step in?" Griff asked.

"She got assistance with heat and food and section nine housing, I think," Carol added. "And I'm sure my dad paid child support, but it probably wasn't close to what she deserved. From the fights I overheard growing up, she was a constant source of conflict for my parents."

"Good old state assistance," I said. "Just dole out the freebies, but don't hold the father accountable."

Griff held up his hand. "Don't start," he said.

He knew better than to get me going on state run programs for women and making taxpayers pick up the pieces while the deadbeat dads walked away.

"I haven't seen him or his mother in years," Carole said. "They sort of faded out of our lives after high school."

Griff shook his head. "It seems like Gwen would have looked for someone a little more laid back after growing up with a father like that."

"The devil you know," I offered.

"Exactly," Carole said. "In Greg's defense he's never touched Gwen. But she can't breathe without asking how much air she should take in. Oddly enough, she's happy with that. She relies on him for everything. She accepts his control and in return she's got the picture-perfect home with the two-point-two kids. Ashley was an incredible success and the world looked favorably on Gwen and her family even if what went on behind the scene wasn't quite the same as what the public saw."

"So as demure as Gwen comes across, she has an agenda?"

"Oh, to be sure. Greg is her agenda."

"You mean keeping him." I said.

Carole nodded. "Or at least maintaining the illusion. Clayton's the only one who ever infiltrated Greg emotionally and after he died, Gwen was sure Greg would leave her. She became obsessed with ways to keep him, not out of love but out of need. It was Ashley who finally drew him out of the world he'd retreated into after losing Clayton, but it was her success that he was enamored with, not his daughter."

"How did Gwen feel about that?" I asked.

"I don't think she cared how he felt or why he became involved with Ashley, as long as he was. Once she saw that Ashley's running was drawing Greg out of his stupor and into the family she'd have moved mountains to make sure Ashley stuck with it."

Carole closed her eyes and shook her head. "She was, is, a good mother. She's just so afraid of being on her own. I wish it wasn't the case. She'd do fine without him, but she has no confidence. For her sake, Greg and I have learned to tolerate each other." She glanced out the window across from our table, her eyes filling. "I don't know if I can do that anymore."

"You blame him?" Griff asked.

"I don't know. I want to, but I'm not sure he deserves it. Clayton's death impacted Ashley as much as it did Greg. She and her brother had been best friends. I mean they both had other kids they hung around with, school chums, but they were close. They complemented each other. Ashley was much like her dad, but in a good way. She had his drive, but also a softer side. Clayton was funny and giving and completely laid-back. Nothing ever riled him, not even his diagnosis. He took it in stride like he did everything else. Even in his final days he was comforting them more than the other way around. And when he was gone, the sun went down for all of them. That was just over five years ago and it hasn't risen since, even though Ashley made it her mission."

"She overcompensated," Griff said.

"Overcompensated doesn't even come close. The girl was driven. She was possessed. The only goal she had in life was to put a smile back on her parents' faces."

"Hence the straight A student, star athlete, acceptance to Johns Hopkins," Griff said.

Carole nodded and waited until the waitress had set our plates in front of us and refilled our coffee before continuing.

"There was nothing she couldn't or wouldn't do."

"And be the best at," I added.

"Not just the best, she had to be miles ahead of her closest competitor in the classroom, on the track, even when it came to her looks. She scoured the magazines for the right clothing, the right make-up, emulating the models' physical appearance until her body gave out and she collapsed weighing in at ninety pounds."

"When was that?" Griff asked scraping his spoon along the inside of his bowl arranging his oatmeal into a center mound.

It was a habit that drove me nuts and I nudged him with my elbow. "Stop," I said, my teeth clenched.

He stifled a smile and nudged me back then keeping his eyes on Carole, "Sorry," he said. "When was that?"

"Just before her high school graduation. She ended up in the Psych unit at Maine Medical Center diagnosed with anorexia, fatigue and dehydration. She didn't attend the ceremony, but she received her diploma. She completed her final exams in the hospital and still aced them."

"How did Greg react to that?"

"He was concerned that if Fensworth found out she'd been hospitalized they'd withdraw her acceptance."

Griff shook his head. "Father of the year."

"Two graduations," I said.

"What's that?" Carole asked draining the last of her coffee.

"She missed two graduations. I mean, she worked her butt off for four years and then misses the payoff both times. What's that mean?"

Carole shrugged. "Ask her shrink."

"Who's that?' Griff asked slipping a notebook and pen from his sport coat pocket.

"Dr. Varkin. He's at Maine Medical Center. I think she was still seeing him off and on until…until she…" Carole bit her lip. "It's hard to say the words, you know? It's like it makes it more real when you say it out loud."

Griff touched her hand. "Take your time."

She picked up her napkin. "I think she was still having sessions until just before she died." She dabbed her eye. "I loved my niece. Maybe that's why I'm telling you. You need to hear this stuff if you're going to figure out what happened, right?"

"Griff nodded. "Absolutely."

"And the asshole will never tell you."

"You think he'll care if we talk to Dr. Varkin?" Griff asked.

"We don't need his permission," I said. "Ashley was an adult."

"I'd like to mention it to him out of respect before we do. He's hired us, after all. Don't want to piss him off."

"I think he'll want you to pursue anything that'll prove she didn't jump from that building," Carole said. "It's a black mark on a perfect life. Greg doesn't like black marks."

I swallowed the dregs of my coffee and looked at her. "I thought his wanting answers came more from a love for his daughter and protecting her legacy."

"Greg is a narcissist. Ashley's success was his success. He took credit for her accomplishments saying he'd raised a miracle child. He loved Ashley the student and Ashley the athlete. I'm not so sure he ever knew Ashley the girl."

"Did Ashley know that?" I asked.

"All she saw was that her achievements made her father happy. She didn't care about much else. After Clayton died her sole purpose was to reinstate happiness into the household." She turned away and wiped her eyes. "Even if it killed her."

"And Gwen?"

"In the beginning, she told Ashley that nothing was going to bring Clayton back. It was a hole that would never be filled. Gwen explained to her that she and Clayton were separate people and one couldn't replace the other. She loved her daughter and couldn't have cared less about ribbons and trophies. But once she saw the effect Ashley's success was having on Greg, she knew it was the key to keeping him. She began fueling Ashley's drive as much as he did."

"Maybe it wasn't only Gwen and Greg's loss," I said. "Maybe Ashley was trying to fill a void within herself too."

Carole looked into her empty coffee cup then up at us and shrugged, her eyes brimming. "We'll never know."

We paid our bill and headed for the parking lot. I couldn't have felt much more despondent, that poor girl, her contradicting mother, her narcissistic father. We hesitated before getting into our cars.

"What now?" Carole asked.

"Talk to Greg, then Varkin," Griff said.

"You know, something keeps bugging me, but I don't want to sound disrespectful. I mean my niece was dedicated, she worked her butt off, but…"

Griff and I waited for her to continue.

"I mean how can a kid be that good? It's not natural. Even in high school she wasn't just at the head of her class she was doing honors classes as a sophomore and not just in one or two subjects, in all of them. And she didn't only win her college races. She won them by minutes not tenths of seconds like in most competitions."

"You mean, you think she might have been using something?" Griff asked.

"Oh, God no. That would never have been her style. She was going for a Masters in Bioethics." Carole shook her head. "It's just, I don't know. How does a kid get that good and stay that good consistently? I have a thirteen-year-old son. He's a B/C student, loves video games and hit a triple last season in baseball. That's his biggest accomplishment so far. And I wouldn't trade him for the world."

Griff shrugged. "Being the best isn't always a good thing. Look where it got Ashley."

Carole nodded. "Thanks for what you're doing. The truth is, we all want to know what happened."

"We'll be in touch," Griff said.

"What do you think?" I asked when we got in the car.

"It's interesting that Carole thinks her niece was a little too good to be true. Most families revel in a kid's success. They don't question it."

"What do you think that means, the fact that she's questioning it?"

"Nothing right now but put it in your back pocket."

SIX

We checked in with Katie. Nothing pressing so we decided to inform Greg of our plan to contact Dr. Varkin.

"You up for another round at Lamberts?" Griff asked slipping his cell phone back into his pocket. He took a left toward the Casco Bay Bridge, connecting Portland to South Portland and Cape Elizabeth.

"Greg agreed to meet with us?"

"Wants to see his money at work."

The house didn't look as foreboding today when we pulled alongside the curb out front. Sunshine works wonders. Greg swung the front door wide and waited for us to reach him before speaking. He was dressed in white shorts and a pink polo shirt that accentuated his tanned skin and defined biceps.

"Heading for the tennis court?" Griff asked.

I think it was tongue in cheek, but Griff's subtle. Sometimes it's hard to tell.

"You play?" Greg asked.

"Never have," Griff said. "Give me a beer and a baseball and I'm happy."

Greg didn't answer, just stepped aside and waved us in.

I swallowed a smile and followed the men into a study off the main entry. An extra-large mahogany desk dominated the room. Greg took the throne behind it. Griff and I slid into matching black leather wingbacks facing him. On either side of us the walls were comprised of floor to ceiling books, interspersed with silver trophies to break up the landscape.

"Yours?" I asked, indicating the trophies.

"Actually, those are Ashley's," he said.

Ashley's trophies on display in Greg's study; apparently, Carole had been right about Gregg accepting Ashley's success as his own. A huge window that took up most of the wall behind him looked onto Gwen's gardens and a perfectly manicured lawn that sloped to a pond complete with ducks.

"Is that Gwen down there?" I asked, seeing someone standing at the water's edge.

Greg glanced over his shoulder and looked back at us. "Lunchtime for the water fowl," he said. "She has to have something to care for." He lowered his eyes for a moment acknowledging the implication of his words. Straightening up he raised his eyebrows. "You said on the phone that you had a question for me."

"After going over my notes last night, I realized I'd forgotten to ask you something," Griff said. "Was Ashley under any kind of medical care or on any medications for physical or mental health?"

At first Greg didn't respond. He took a deep breath and studied his wedding band as he rolled it around his finger. "What makes you think that?" he asked looking up.

"If she was, it could be important."

"Because?" Greg kept his eyes on Griff, still fiddling with his ring,

Griff shifted in is seat. "Mr. Lambert, a person in good mental and physical health doesn't jump off a building. Ashley seemed to be at the pinnacle of both, which is what makes her suicide so hard to accept. Thinking about that last night, I began to wonder if there was something underlying her success, some illness or obstacle she was trying to overcome."

"Ashley lost her brother almost six years ago. Since then, she's seen a psychiatrist whenever she felt the need."

"I'm sorry to hear that," Griff said. "It must make Ashley's death that much more unbearable."

"Greg nodded. "Dr. Varkin," he said. "I don't know his exact location; my wife made all the arrangements."

"Were you in agreement that Ashley should see a psychiatrist?" I asked picking up the indifference in his voice.

"No one in my family has needed mental health professionals, but I believe there've been a few on my wife's side who've required such services. I decided since that was something my wife was familiar with she should be the one to handle it. We didn't discuss it."

Scar Tissue

I glanced at Griff. Strike three. Could I kill him now?

Griff looked at me and shook his head slightly, indicating he'd read my mind and the answer was, no.

"His office is in Portland?" Griff asked.

"I believe so. Is that all you need from me today?" Greg pushed his chair back and stood, checking his watch indicating he was done.

"That's it," Griff said. It won't be an issue for you if we speak with him?"

"Doesn't matter to me. Might be an issue for him. Doctor patient privilege and all that." I'll phone him and call you."

"Appreciate it."

Greg led us to the front door without another word and pulled it wide. Sunshine spilled onto the cold marble floor.

"Thanks for your time," Griff said, and we stepped outside onto the flagstone walkway.

The door closed behind us.

"Whoa," I said. "Do you think he's a dick all the time or just when he's talking to us?"

"He likes to be in control. That's why he said he'll call Varkin and let us know."

"We don't need him to be the go-between."

"We don't. He does."

Griff raised the key fob and the 1975 Series III Land Rover chirped back at him, unlocking the doors as we approached.

"You locked it? You think somebody in this neighborhood would want your geriatric ride?" I laughed.

"Geriatric? She's aged like fine wine."

"You got the aged part right."

"Hey, you shouldn't be throwing stones. I bought her because you wanted my two-year-old Rav."

"You bought her because she's the car of your dreams. And you've invested more in your four-wheeled girlfriend than most people would consider worthwhile."

"Am I detecting a note of jealousy?"

"Skepticism, of installing a new engine, leather interior, a state-of-the-art computer and a security system in a forty-year-old car."

"Not just any forty-year-old car, an antique Land Rover. And she may well outlive the Rav with all the upgrades I've made."

"Something to look forward to," I said and slid onto the refurbished front seat.

"Let's pay Gina a visit before we hook up with Varkin," Griff said veering onto High Street toward downtown Portland.

"She did the autopsy?"

"We'll find out."

Gina Wellington used to be the state Medical Examiner, but after the birth of her second child she'd opened a private practice as a family physician. She still performed autopsies when the Chief Medical Examiner in Augusta was facing cadaver overload. (Okay, that's gross, but it happens.) It was our good luck that she'd settled in the Portland area, saving us the drive to Augusta every time we needed her expertise.

"Haven't seen you two in a while," Gina said looking up from where she stood behind her receptionist. "Be right with you." She slipped off black-rimmed glasses and smiled at the man and child in front of her. "Follow up in two weeks," she said to the dad, brushing back an ebony coil that had escaped her barrette.

I had the feeling fathers were more than happy to bring their kids in for check-ups when their doctors looked like they'd stepped off a page of Vogue or Cosmo.

With a wave, Gina motioned for us to follow and we fell in step down the oriental carpeted hallway, past exam room doors and into her office.

"So," she said taking the seat behind her desk. "What can I do for you? Wait a minute." She held up her hand. "First things first. How have you been? I haven't seen either of you for quite a while. Still in business, I hope?"

"Oh yeah," Griff said glancing at me. "Our last case took us up north and then over the border, so we haven't been around much."

"All good?" Gina asked.

Griff's hesitancy was obvious. It wasn't a case either of us discussed except with each other. And then it was relegated to under the covers in the wee hours of morning when painful memories are purged in whispers.

"All good," Griff said and then changed the subject. "We're buying a house."

"That's big news. Where?"

We gave her a virtual tour right down to the exercise room and mini bar.

"I'll wait for an invitation, but I want to see this place in person," she said when we'd finished.

"It's a party place alright," Griff told her. "My daughter is already making a guest list."

She laughed. "So, what brings you to my humble office?"

"Ashley Lambert," I said.

The smile faded from Gina's face. She shook her head. "Tragic."

"Suicide?" I asked.

She looked at me and raised her eyebrows. "You don't think so?"

"We've been hired by her parents to find out."

"Her father pushed for an autopsy at the time of her death."

"He did?"

"Said there was no way she jumped. He was sure someone had killed her first then tossed her off the building to make it look like suicide."

"Did you do the autopsy?" I asked.

"We did the best we could. There's not a lot to work with after a fall from eighteen stories. I don't think her father realized that and I didn't want to be the one to explain to him what a fall like that does to the human body. The mother was distraught and against the whole idea. She couldn't bear her daughter's body being cut up. I didn't want to tell her it was in pieces when I got it. But the state stepped in and took it out of the parents' hands anyway."

"The state didn't think it was suicide?"

"There was some question. And her father was putting up quite a stink. I couldn't blame him. But regardless of who thought what, it was an un-witnessed, violent death. That gets the ME's attention. The mother felt it wasn't worth it. It looked like a straightforward suicide, but Mack ordered an autopsy, at least as much of one as we could do."

"The Medical Examiner can do that, even if one parent doesn't want it?" I asked.

"In a violent death like that, yes. And if there's a remote chance of foul play or drugs involved then it's pretty much mandatory. Ashley had so much going for her that her manner of death did raise some questions."

"Find anything?" Griff asked.

She shook her head. "It would have been next to impossible with the extent of the damage to her body. By the time we'd finished there was still no reason to think anything, but the fall killed her."

"Did you do a drug screen?" Griff asked.

"Standard 5 panel, but it's not back yet. Four to six weeks, nobody gets special treatment."

"Not even when they have the Lamberts' money?"

"The lab doesn't care about money unless it's coming in as funding."

"Lambert say anything about the fact that a drug panel was being done?" I asked.

"He said it was a waste of time. I explained that it might not be necessary, but it's part of a standard autopsy. When I'm dealing with a parent I don't argue. I let them take the lead and I answer their questions. Rarely, do I offer unsolicited information. The conversation is difficult enough. I give them whatever they ask for, but not more. If they have questions they can call me later."

"Has he?"

She shook her head.

"Could she have had something in her system that wouldn't show up?" I asked. "Something that could have caused her to think irrationally or become suicidal?"

Gina nodded. "Sure. But my guess is that it would have to be something she'd been taking over time. I mean a kid tries cocaine once for example, they're not going to be suicidal, but ingest something long term and it can change brain chemistry. You think she was using something?"

"It's an angle worth considering," Griff said.

"From what I've heard she doesn't sound like the type. But if she was using, it'll depend on the substance itself as to whether or not it shows up."

"How so?"

"Well, for example, amphetamines can only be detected in the blood for 12-24 hours. There are other tests using hair or urine that provide more in-depth results, but Ashley's been cremated. Because no one was thinking drugs, there was no reason to hold her body. It was released to a funeral home after the autopsy. Unless she'd had a big race the day before she jumped, or she was using consistently, I doubt we'll see anything in the amphetamine realm if you're thinking performance enhancers. But who knows, a tox screen can be full of surprises."

I looked at Griff and tried not to let the dimple on his left cheek side track me. It always appeared when he got excited over a theory and was stifling a grin. Which told me he liked the direction the case had taken. Drugs, even the possibility of drugs in her system made sense and gave us our first indication that Ashley Lambert may have been something other than the miracle child her parents described.

I turned back to Gina. "She was under tremendous stress physically and academically. A boost to get her through the day makes sense."

"Doesn't sound like it from her parents' description."

"Maybe it's time to stop talking to family," I said. "How many kids show their true self to mom and dad? I sure as hell didn't."

"Two things I've learned in this job," Gina said. "One is that anything's possible. And two, there's a way around everything. You just have to know how to get there."

Griff's cell phone rang. Our conversation stopped.

"Yeah, okay. Thank you. We'll be in touch." He hit the red circle on the bottom of his phone and dropped it back into the pocket of his sport coat. "That was Greg. We have the green light for Dr. Varkin." he said.

"Steven Varkin as in Psychiatrist?" Gina asked.

"That's the one. He was Ashley's shrink. Greg just opened the door for us to talk to him."

"He's good. Hope he can help you more than I did."

"Maybe Dr. Varkin can shed some light on the question of Ashley's drug use, prescription or otherwise," Griff said. "Let us know when you get the toxicology report."

"Will do," Gina said swinging the door wide. "If it shows up positive for drugs you'll be faced with a can of worms."

"Yeah," I said. "One that needs to be opened."

SEVEN

We arranged to meet with Dr. Varkin at six o'clock. With time to kill we went for an early dinner at Conundrum, our favorite stomping ground when working a case. (The name says it all.) We took a seat at one of the high tops in the bar.

"The usual," Griff said to Eric when he approached.

"You got it." The waiter turned and headed for the bar.

Griff stretched his legs out beneath the table, resting his heels on the metal rim around my stool. The toe of his worn Frye boot grazed my shin.

"What do we have so far?" he asked as Eric set a Pinot Grigio and Black Fly Stout in front of us.

I took a sip. (First things first.) "Controlling father, weak, but loving mother, dead brother and an overachieving kid. Reeks of suicide." I took another sip.

Griff raised his mug, swallowed a third of the dark beer and wiped his mouth with the back of his hand. He looked across the table and narrowed his brown eyes at me."

My heart skipped a beat. "Cut the shit," I said.

"What?"

I shook my head. "Nothing." I love westerns and Griff has the indifferent cowboy look down. He's the stranger who saunters into town, takes out the local miscreant for getting rough with a girl then pulls her onto the horse behind him and off they go into the sunset.

"Getting back on track…" I said.

"I didn't know we'd gotten off."

I waved him away with the back of my hand. "I think she was cracking under pressure, her own and her father's. I think she needed a little boost to keep her going and maybe her boost got out of hand."

Eric set a plate of seafood nachos between us.

"But we don't know that anything will come back on the drug screen," Griff pointed out.

"Gina said herself there are things that go undetected."

"Greg Lambert won't be thrilled when we tell him that's the angle we're pursuing. Puts the possibility of a black mark on his perfect daughter.

"Hey, you're the one that came up with this, remember?"

"Maybe we're jumping the gun with a drug theory."

"That's the father in you talking. This is the first theory we've had, and I think you're onto something. Let's play with it." I sipped my Pinot. It was going down way too easy. "Then again, if she was taking something and it doesn't show up on the tox screen it'll be almost impossible to prove. We could smear her and never be able to confirm the theory. If that happens Daddy's not going to be pleased with us."

"I think he knows suicide is the cause of death," Griff said. "But he's reluctant to accept it until he gets the *why*. If we pursue the drug use narrative, we may be able to get an answer for him. Even if it's one he doesn't like."

"He's not gonna like any *why* we give him." I stuffed a chip laden with salsa, cheese and scallops into my mouth and sat back to enjoy.

"Probably not. Hopefully Varkin will tell us that he prescribed a bunch of drugs, they interacted and she jumped."

"That's a nice, neat little package and places the fault on Varkin not Ashley. Greg would be pleased. But again…what if nothing shows up?"

"You gotta ruin everything, don't you?"

At five-fifty-five we stepped inside Dr. Varkin's waiting room. At six o'clock he opened his door. Tall, as in the NBA's Dwight Howard tall, late sixties and lean as a marathoner, he extended his hand. "Mr. Cole," he said. "Ms. Callahan."

We followed him into a room tailor made for comfort. Recliners, couches and beanbag chairs offered themselves to the mentally weary. Griff and I settled side by side on a couch. Dr. Varkin draped his frame over a red leather recliner.

"Greg Lambert said you had some questions regarding Ashley. Why don't you ask, and I'll answer?"

"We've just come from Dr. Gina Wellington's office," Griff said. "She performed the autopsy but found nothing that ruled out the initial summation of suicide by jumping. With all Ashley's accomplishments, the family is having a tough time accepting that as cause of death, understandably so. Do you have any reason to think she may have been using drugs?"

Dr. Varkin looked surprised. He shook his head. "No, I have no reason to think Ashley was using drugs of any kind. I'd often suggested an anti-depressant but she always refused. She was afraid it would interfere with her athletics. She may have been right about that so I didn't push it, though I think it would have been helpful given her issues."

"Her issues," I said. "Can you elaborate?"

"I first saw Ashley when she was in high school. Shortly after her brother died. She was distraught, as would be expected. As time went on, she got worse rather than better."

"She couldn't accept his death?" Griff asked.

"She understood he was ill and it was beyond anyone's control. But she was never allowed time to grieve. Gwen had a complete breakdown. She was in bed for the better part of a year. Greg, shut down, lived in his own world. Ashley was left to her own devices. The emotional absence of both parents at a time when she was in great need of their love and support caused her to slip toward self-destructive behavior."

"Self-destructive?" I asked.

"Well," he shifted his position, uncrossed his legs and planted his wingtips on the floor. With his elbows on his knees he looked directly at me. "I called it self-destructive. Greg would probably call it meeting expectations. Running track was a metaphor for Ashley. If she slowed down enough to look at what was going on in her life, she would have collapsed."

"Like her parents did," I said.

Dr. Varkin nodded, "Exactly. She kept moving because they couldn't. And she was quite good at it, though initially, maybe twenty pounds overweight."

"Overweight? She looked fit from the pictures I've seen," Griff said.

"From what she told me in our sessions, she was overweight as a child and carried excess weight into high school. Clayton died in her junior year, that's when things began to change."

"Kids gave her grief for being fat?" I asked.

"Not kids, her father. She became obsessed with pleasing him. And she didn't stay overweight for long. Within a year of Clayton's death, her athletic success caught Greg's interest and from then on Ashley lived under his microscope. He put her on a diet regimen that would challenge even a professional runner. But Ashley stuck to it verbatim. She would not disappoint. In her eyes, the family had suffered enough. If her running alleviated their despair then she'd have run to the moon and back if she could."

"What did Gwen think of all this?"

"At first Gwen thought Ashley was working too hard, though she did little to intervene."

"Because Gwen wasn't taking care of herself then," I said. "She was still in bed wasn't she?"

Varkin nodded. "Most of the time. But she was right. Ashley was working too hard, obsessed with pleasing them. The thinner she was the faster she ran and the faster she ran the happier Greg was. Halfway through her senior year of high school I had her admitted to Maine Medical Center's Psych ward. She was anorexic, depressed, dehydrated and exhausted."

"What did Greg have to say about that?"

She'd been accepted at Fensworth as a student and a member of the Women's Track and Field Team. I think he was more concerned that her hospital admittance would put that in jeopardy than he was about his daughter's health.

He never visited her. By that time, Gwen was back on her feet. She'd sold her nursery and spent most of her time landscaping the grounds of their home. But she visited Ashley every day for the three weeks of her admittance. Like everything else, Ashley put all her energy into getting well and she excelled at it. She began nutrition classes and continued them throughout that summer. She never slipped into anorexia again, but her eating became as controlled as the rest of her life. As soon as she was discharged Greg put her on a rigorous training schedule."

"And everything went back to the way it was?" I asked.

Dr. Varkin nodded. I saw Ashley off and on throughout her undergraduate years. Nothing much changed. She pushed herself beyond what her mind and body could support on a daily basis."

"She pushed herself or her parents did?" Griff asked.

"In truth, they were both so entangled in Ashley, it was hard to know where one ended and the other began. One of the unhealthiest parent/child relationships I've seen short of abuse."

"You said Gwen felt Ashley needed to take better care of herself."

"Initially, yes, when Ashley was in the hospital. But her concern changed once she saw how involved Greg was becoming. Ashley was receiving a slew of mixed messages from her mother. Gwen was out of bed and happy again, smiling at the finish line. That alone outweighed any health issues Ashley was dealing with."

"The ultimate example of codependency," I said. "Guess I'm lucky my parents didn't give a damn."

"We all have our demons."

"And Greg?" I asked before Dr. Varkin tried to schedule me an appointment.

"Greg wanted glory at any cost." The doctor rubbed his fingers over the gray stubble on his chin. "You must realize that you are dealing with a very disturbed family. Their relationships toward one another are, or were, toxic. They feed each other's illnesses."

"But Ashley never took drugs, prescription or otherwise that you know of?" Griff asked.

"None that came from this office and she never mentioned taking anything to me."

"Do you think she would have?" I asked. "I mean, told you if she were."

Varkin pursed his lips and exhaled through his nose. He looked at the rug beneath his feet for a few moments weighing his answer. "No, she may not have told me. To her, that would have meant she was flawed. It would have been a secret she buried so deep I doubt anyone will ever uncover it."

We thanked the doctor for his time and walked to the elevator down the hall from his office. "Jesus," I said. "I'm exhausted from listening to him describe Ashley's lifestyle. I can't imagine actually living it."

"It's frightening how much influence parents have over how their kids turn out. Every decision from the moment they're born impacts who they'll become." Griff shook his head, "If you really think about it, it could scare people right out of procreating."

"Natural birth control," I said. "Not a bad idea."

We stopped in front of the elevators and when the doors opened, stepped inside.

"Not everyone screws up their kids," he said. Look at Allie. She's awesome."

"No argument there. But we just bought a house. One step at a time."

"So, what's our next step?" he asked. "A puppy?"

"To figure out what happened to Ashley."

"You're sidestepping."

"But not back peddling."

The doors opened. "Guess I'll quit while I'm ahead," he said.

EIGHT

The next morning Peggy called. The house inspection was scheduled for ten o'clock.

"Guess that means we're taking the day off," I said pouring a second cup of coffee. "Okay if Amy joins us? She hasn't seen the house yet."

"Sure, I don't think it'll matter if she's there for the inspection."

My sister Amy is my best friend. We're very different and I think that's why we're as close as we are. She's traditional and careful, while I tend to put my head in the lion's mouth. Amy and I raised each other because my parents had better things to do. Being two years older, Amy took on the role of the parent. I opted to be a child. We're still connected at the hip, hearts in harmony.

"I was thinking we'd go have a talk with Ashley's running coach at Fensworth," Griff said. "But I suppose it can wait one more day."

"He's there now? Isn't the semester over?"

"The Athletic Department said sports camps run all summer. Coach Massett is on the track from nine to one. I'm going to take a shower." He stopped in the doorway. "Join me?"

I looked at the cup of coffee I'd just poured and then back at Griff. No contest. I got up and followed him into the bathroom. There's nothing like having someone wash your hair. It could be my favorite part of showering together. And by the time it's done I'm relaxed, loose and yielding. I think that's Griff's favorite part.

We turned into the driveway and stopped before reaching the house.

Hesitating beneath the overhang of trees, we admired our almost house with its farmers' porch and red metal roof.

"In a few weeks this will be ours," Griff said.

I squeezed his hand. "I love you."

He leaned over the stick shift and kissed me, sealing the deal.

Pulling forward, we came to a stop beside Peggy's car just as a pick-up

truck lumbered down the driveway. The lettering on the side of the vehicle read Hughes Home Inspections.

"This generally takes a while," Steve Hughes explained. "Feel free to follow me around and ask questions or I'll find you when I'm done and we can review."

Griff stuffed his hands into the front pockets of his jeans. "I'll follow if you don't mind."

I caught sight of Amy's Subaru turning in at the end if the driveway. "I'll wait for her." I said, nodding toward the approaching car. "We'll catch up."

The men started in the garage. Not high on my list of interesting places so I opened the front door and stepped into the living room. The previous owners had agreed to leave whatever we wanted with the house. We'd negotiated the worth and added it to the asking price. Still a steal, these people really wanted out. It bothered me somewhat that they were in so much of a hurry. I couldn't shake the feeling they were running away from something.

"Hey there," Amy said coming through the open front door. "Can I just say, wow? Is that enough to tell you what I think of this place so far?"

"Where's Caleb?"

"Day care. I dropped him for a couple hours, so I could go for a run and pick up groceries without having to buy a bunch of junky, bribe food."

"You're no fun," I said.

"Just wait till you're a mom, little sister."

"Don't hold your breath. Follow me. You ain't seen nothin' yet."

I gave Amy the full tour, starting in the kitchen. She ran her hand the length of the oak table and emitted the appropriate wow again. We moved to the second floor, the guest room and master bedroom. She stepped into the glassed-in shower stall, her sneakers squeaking against the tile, and looked into the forest of trees beyond. "You know that only a true psycho would hide in those woods to watch you shower, right?"

"Really? That hadn't occurred to me, but thanks. I'll keep it in mind when I'm standing in here naked."

We stepped onto the balcony off the master bedroom and descended the stairs to the deck. Amy peered into the weight room.

"Go ahead," I said. Twenty minutes on the elliptical. You're already dressed for it."

She shook her head, her blond ponytail swinging against the middle of her back. "Rain check. I promised Caleb I'd be back for him in two hours." She checked her watch. "My time as a free woman is almost up."

"He's four years old. He can't tell time."

"Yeah, but I can and I keep my promises. I'll be back as soon as you guys move in. In fact, you're gonna get sick of me."

"Not a chance."

I walked her to her car.

"How're the neighbors?" she asked nodding toward the McKenzie's roof that could be seen above the trees.

"Okay, I think. He's a cop in Portland."

"Griff know him?"

"No, most of Griff's cohorts are in the detective unit. He doesn't know the uniforms. She's pregnant, due in a couple of months. She seemed a little weird, but it's hard to know the first time you meet someone."

"Never judge a woman whose hormones are holding her captive. I'm sure she'll be fine." Lines etched across Amy's forehead. "McKenzie. They're not the people...."

"Whose kid disappeared? Yeah, they are."

"Jesus, you're moving in next door?"

"They're not murderers. They lost their child. I feel sorry for them."

"I always thought he did it. I think most people did, but they never proved anything."

"Griff didn't say that."

"Contrary to your belief, Griff doesn't know everything."

"He seems like a nice guy."

"They all do, until…" She ran her finger across her throat. "At least you have plenty of buffer between you." She nodded toward the tree line.

"Get out of here. Go take care of your kid and count your blessings that you

have him. Some people aren't so lucky."

"I'll bring champagne next time." She slipped onto her front seat and started the engine.

"And bring Caleb. Griff needs a fix," I added.

I watched Amy disappear down the driveway, glanced at the mini forest separating our land from McKenzie's and went back inside. I could hear Griff and Steve in the basement talking about the furnace. Nothing I cared about so I headed for the second floor. In the master bedroom, I laid across the king size bed and watched clouds drift past the skylight. Lazy Sunday mornings with breakfast in bed would be a priority, at least until kids sabotaged the peace. Kids…the thought surprised me. Children were something I rarely considered. At thirty-three, I still had plenty of time and since men can procreate until their dying breath, Griff was in his prime at forty-five. Amy says Caleb's her life, but when I look at the Ashley Lamberts of the world and see the destruction a parent can cause even when they don't mean to, parenting scares the shit out of me. I'm in no rush.

In the bathroom, I put my palms against the floor to ceiling glass wall of the shower and thought about Amy's comment on psychos. Through the trees I could just see the McKenzie's house. Only their rooftop was visible. I wondered what the view was like when the leaves were off the trees. At least then I'd be able to watch the psychos while they watched me. Before I could give it more thought, something moved beneath me in the yard. Rhea McKenzie stepped from the tree line. She emerged from the path I could now see from my overhead vantage point, a narrow trail snaking from one house to the other.

I stepped out of the master bedroom onto the small balcony.

"Hi," she said as I descended the stairs connecting the balcony to the deck below.

"Hi."

"Home inspection today?" she asked.

I nodded, "Yeah."

"They're pretty boring. Thought you might like to come over for some iced tea, while the men scrounge around with wires and pipes."

I laughed. She seemed nothing like the mousy woman I'd met a few days ago, her husband leading her around by the arm. I remembered what Amy had said about ravaging hormones. "I'd love to," I said.

I followed her through the trees back the way she'd come, on the path between the two houses.

"Did you and…I don't know the name of the people who lived here, but did you visit each other often? The path looks well worn."

"Their name was Morrow, Ellen and Mitch, and no we didn't visit much. At first we did, but after…after a while that stopped. Except for Halsey. She and I met whenever we could."

"Halsey?"

"Their daughter. She's five."

"Do you have other children?" I asked before thinking. She hesitated and looked at me and then slowly shook her head. "No," she said.

I let it go.

We emerged at the edge of a chain link gate that surrounded the pool. Rhea flipped up the horseshoe clip and the gate swung open. "Have a seat." She gestured toward the patio furniture. "I'll be right back."

She climbed a set of stone steps and disappeared inside the French doors.

The back of their house was almost entirely glass. Kitchen on the right where I could see Rhea moving around and a living room to the left where I could make out a large flat screen television hanging on the wall above a fireplace and a circular black leather couch. Not bad for a beat cop.

Rhea appeared holding a tray with two tall glasses of iced tea, lemon wedges and a plate of butter cookies.

I reached for a glass, squeezed in lemon and took a sip. "Thanks," I said. "I didn't realize how warm it was getting." I slipped onto one of the canvas loungers and kicked off my sandals.

"Finally," she said. "I wait all winter for the day I can open the pool and then spend every minute out here, breakfast to dinner." She folded her pink and white cover-up over the back of the other lounge chair and took a seat stretching out long thin legs and rubbing her palm absently over her baby bulge.

"How do you feel?" I asked nodding toward her stomach.

"Good," she said smiling, but her smile faded too quickly. "Most of the time."

She got up and walked to the edge of the pool. Bending her right knee, she swished a toe through the sparkling blue water.

I was glad her back was to me because I couldn't have hidden my surprise. The skin on her back was discolored with varying shades of blue and yellow, bruises, new and old. On the side of her thigh was a deep purple circle the size of a fist.

She turned around fast like she'd suddenly remembered I was there and now privy to what had previously been hidden. She lifted her pool robe from the back of her chair, slipped into it and sat, all the time watching my face.

When I'd worked in Family Law, bruises like Rhea's were a routine occurrence, but it had been four years since I'd left that world. For a while I'd kept my foot in the door offering free legal aid to women in violent relationships. But when Griff and I worked a case where women I'd had contact with kept turning up dead I stopped. Bad juju.

Rhea took a breath. "I fell," she said.

It was clear from her voice that even she knew her explanation sounded lame.

I nodded. "Looks like it was a bad one."

"Yeah," she said. "It was."

We both knew what was happening, but we'd also just met. It wasn't time for her to divulge long kept secrets or for me to pursue them.

"Your home is beautiful," I said nodding toward the glassed back of the house. Mike does well as a cop."

"Oh," she smiled and looked down at her hands in her lap. "He has a little help. His parents left a trust. At least I think that's what it is. I'm not sure. He handles the finances."

"You're lucky. I'm not sure my parents have ever given me more than bus fare. And that was just to get me out of the house."

Rhea's laugh was throaty and sensual. She had a beautiful smile, full and strong with straight white teeth. And in that moment, I saw an entirely different woman than the one I'd met with Mike the other night.

"You and Halsey were friends?" I asked.

"Yeah," She nodded. "We were good friends. I loved her company and I think she felt the same way. We planted a garden last year." She pointed to a small square of dirt where sparse weeds and decaying leaves flourished. "I didn't have the heart to start it again this spring once I knew they were leaving."

"Sounds like you'll miss her."

"I will, very much even though I didn't get to see her very often anymore. Ellen didn't like her to come over here. In the beginning, when we'd first moved in we got together quite a lot, but after…"

Her voice trailed off and she looked at me as though she'd lost her train of thought or maybe just didn't want to continue. I waited to see if she was going to explain about her son's disappearance.

"Ellen and I were good friends and our…I mean Halsey came over a lot, but after…after a while, I guess they made other friends. I didn't see them much. They always seemed to have other plans. Occasionally she'd let Halsey come over, but I don't think Mitch liked it."

"Why not?"

She shrugged. "He and Mike didn't have much in common. Ellen and I connected right away, but…I guess it takes longer for men."

She didn't elaborate, and I let it go…for now. "So, that's how the path came to be?"

Rhea let go with her rich, warm laugh again and I found myself smiling just hearing it.

"Yeah, Ellen and I cleared it together early on and then Halsey and I maintained it. She'd come over in the morning and we'd pack a lunch and go outside to work. We'd take a break at noontime and sit in the dirt and eat. I think she loved doing that. What kid doesn't like to play in the dirt?"

"What changed Ellen's mind?"

Rhea shrugged. "I don't know. She just seemed to get uncomfortable."

I sat silently for a moment wondering if I should push her but decided against it. There was plenty of time to dig. "Maybe she was jealous of the fact that Halsey liked being with you."

Rhea looked into my eyes and smiled. "Yeah," she said. "Maybe that was it."

"I'm sorry. Sometimes I shoot my mouth off a little more than I should. Well, make that a lot more. Comes with the job."

"It's okay. Mike does the same thing. I understand. Anyway, it's nice to have someone to talk to again."

Griff emerged from the same path we'd taken. "There you are. Peggy thought she'd seen you disappear into the trees." He nodded to Rhea. "Nice to see you again."

"Tea?" she asked raising her glass.

"Not this time. I think we're ready to go, Britt. Everything looks good."

I stood. "Thanks for the tea."

"It's the first of many, I hope," Rhea said.

I smiled. "Definitely."

I followed Griff out the gate and we wound our way through the woods.

"She seemed different today than last time," he said. "Was she?"

"Night and day."

"How come?"

I considered telling him about the discolored skin on her back and my suspicions, but it was just a guess at this point, an educated one, but still a guess. Griff hated it when I jumped to conclusions.

"Amy said it's hormones. And some women are different when their husbands are around."

"Why's that?"

I thought of Rhea's bruises. "Depends on the guy."

He turned and looked at me, clearly confused.

"You have nothing to worry about," I said and waved him on down the path.

NINE

David Hughes of Hughes Home Inspection left us with a handshake and a three-ringed binder that provided a detailed report of our soon to be new home. He'd suggested minor repairs, but nothing that would leave our bank account violated. Now it was wait-it-out time, while the bank did its vetting of us, scrutinizing every last penny we earned and spent and decided if we were a good investment. I wasn't worried.

Griff checked his watch. "You up for a trip to Fensworth? Coach Massett should still be on the field."

After a pit stop at Panara Bread (there's nothing better than their iced green tea) we pulled onto the Fensworth College campus. Passing beneath a wrought iron archway we approached Admissions, a Greek revival complete with massive columns lining a wide veranda that stretched end to end across the front of the building. Beyond that, were the classrooms and the quad. A compilation of Federal and Greek style architecture surrounding a garden with picnic benches and lawns sufficient for an afternoon game of Frisbee. The campus was impressive if a bit intimidating. We followed a narrow drive threading through dormitory buildings and followed signs to the athletic complex. Emerging into a parking lot fit for an NFL event, Griff let out a whistle. A playing field surrounded by an eight-lane track lay beyond the chain link fence.

"I didn't know Fensworth athletics drew large enough crowds for a complex this size."

"They don't, but they like to think they do," Griff said.

"Expensive ego."

"That's one way to put it."

"Aren't they small for Division 1 athletics?"

"They're not D1 in everything. Track and Ice Hockey, I think."

We parked along the fence and watched three runners make the turn in front of us heading for the hurdles.

The coach gave us half a glance as we approached. "Help you folks?" he asked keeping one eye on his runners.

"Coach Massett?" Griff asked.

"Let me guess. You have a daughter who runs and you're doing the college search. Well, I'll tell you, my girls are number one in the state. Tenth in the nation."

"Not in the market, yet," Griff said. "My daughter's fifteen."

"Never too soon," Massett said. "Getting noticed is a bitch."

We offered him our IDs. He glanced at them uninterested.

"We were hoping to talk with you about Ashley Lambert," Griff said.

That got his attention. He shook his head and blew out a quick puff of air. "Now there's a tragedy. What the hell happened?"

"That's what we've been hired to find out. In your opinion, was she having any problems academically or…" Griff nodded toward the track, "here?"

"She was obsessed. Had to be the best and she was. I've never had any kid with a work ethic like hers. I almost wanted her to take it down a notch, ya know? Not something you'd hear from a coach very often, but Ashley worried me at times."

"Worried you how?" I asked.

He shrugged. "I don't know. Sometimes she seemed a little off balance. Up here." He tapped his index finger against the side of his head. "Liked to talk, what girl doesn't? But Jesus, she could ramble on and on about nothing. I learned to tune her out. Can't really put my finger on it, but she seemed like she was moving too fast. Christ, some days I was scared she'd drop of a heart attack. But she kept going."

He stepped a foot or two toward the track. "Again," he yelled as the three runners passed us. "Step it up."

"Was the energy something new?"

"She'd ended the spring season with the number two runners closing in. Her times weren't quite what they had been, but they were still good enough to keep her in the number one position. Then at summer training camp she seemed a little edgy. I asked her if she was okay. She chalked it up to too much coffee. But I mentioned it to her father. Not that he gave a shit as long as her finish times were good. And they were."

"And it was worse recently?" I asked.

"Yeah, it was the same when she came back to school in September and practices started up again. There was a nervous energy about her, twitchy, but she was at the top of her game. Best runner I've ever had. Same in the classroom. Whatever was going on with her didn't affect her ability."

"Did you ask her about drugs?"

He looked at me obviously offended. "My girls are in top form because they work hard. We don't need any boosts on this team."

"Do you test before a race?"

"I don't, but the NCAA does random testing at tournaments."

"Ever get a positive?" I asked.

"Never, not even one in the eleven years I've been here. My girls are solid. What you see is what you get."

"She ever tell you anything in confidence?" I asked. "Trouble at home?"

He shook his head. "I think her father was pretty tough on her, but she never complained. At least not to me."

Coach Massett checked the stop-watch in his hand then lifted his gaze to the runners on the far side of the track.

We waited.

He took a step to the side, bumped into me and looked up like he was surprised I was still there. He glanced from me to Griff and realized we were waiting for more.

"Her father hung around behind the bench no matter how many times I'd ask him to stay in the stands with the other parents. Thought his money spoke louder than theirs. He was a pain in my ass, to put it bluntly. Always coaching her, pushing her. That's what they pay me for. And like she needed anyone to do that, anyway. The kid had the drive of a grizzly in mating season."

"What about friends? Was there anyone on the team she was close to?"

"More the opposite. My girls are competitive, not just with our rival schools but with each other. As much as this is a team it's a team of individuals. Every one of them wants the top score, but it was Ashley's every time. I think the others were resentful, sick of her always being the one in the spotlight. Can't blame 'em, but it made the rest of them work like hell."

The runners flew past us again, legs stretching out in front of them, arms pumping.

"Last lap," Coach yelled.

"That's her roommate." He pointed to the woman leading the trio. "Mitzi Gannon. Don't think there was much love lost when Ashley died. Mitzi's here on scholarship after being home schooled kindergarten to high school by her Born Again parents. She's a bit awkward socially and breaking the tape on the heels of a pretty, rich girl really crawled up her ass. The casket had barely been lowered and she was out here on the track with the finish line in sight. She's finally got the chance to be the first one across and she's workin' her butt off to make it happen."

"What're her chances?" Griff asked.

"Excellent. She's a hell of a runner."

"Mind if we talk to her for a minute when she comes in?"

"Be my guest."

The girls came off the track hands on hips, heads down sucking in air. They each grabbed a water bottle off the bench before walking up and down the sideline to catch their breath.

Griff and I flanked Mitzi.

"Nice run," I said.

She nodded and wiped at the sweat dripping off her nose with the back of her hand.

I tried to remember the last time I'd exercised or run that was not related to chasing down some asshole. I think I was ten. That's not to say I'm in bad shape. I might be nearing mid-thirties, but at five-eight, one-twenty, I can still turn heads. And Griff's not complaining. That's all that matters.

"We're investigating the death of Ashley Lambert and understand you were her roommate," Griff said.

Mitzi stopped and took a gulp of water. "Not by choice. We weren't friends. The school stuck us together. I guess they thought since we both ran track we'd be a good match." She shrugged.

"But..." I said hoping to lead her on.

"But nothing. We lived together. We weren't friends. That's pretty much it. We didn't hang out or anything."

"Were you surprised by her suicide?"

"Everybody was." She picked up a towel and rubbed the back of her neck.

"Did she seem off in any way in the days before she died?"

"She was always "off". She was a weirdo. She was one big stressed-out, control freak. Every day was exactly the same. Up at the same time every morning, ate the same breakfast, went to class, the library, practice, dinner, study, sleep. Well, if you could call it sleep. More like sleepwalking. I'd wake up in the middle of the night and there she'd be, puttering around the room, putting away clothes or organizing her desk. Drove me crazy."

"Parties?"

Mitzi shook her head. "No way. A party or socializing didn't fit into her schedule."

"Did she have any friends?" I asked.

"None that I ever saw. She was always alone except when her parents were around. They came to everything, even practices. Her father was as crazy as she was."

"Like what?"

"Sometimes I'd hear them talking on the way back to our room after practice or an event. He'd be harping on how important winning was. As soon as one race was over they were already discussing the next one and how imperative it was that she won. Ashley would just keep nodding her head, agreeing. I mean, she'd have just beat the hell out of her opponents and instead of congratulating her, her father would be telling her to gear up for the next one. It's no wonder Ashley killed herself. I would too with a father like that."

"What about her mother?"

"She was always there too, but she never said much other than to tell Ashley to keep it up. But she was a weirdo too."

"How so?" I asked.

"It was just the way she talked to her. Like, she never sounded encouraging, more like her life depended on it."

"Did Ashley have any losses or setbacks the week she died?"

"I wish."

I glanced at Griff. Mitzi's compassion was underwhelming. "Her parents have picked up her belongings from the dorm room, I assume?"

"Her aunt came and picked up her stuff a couple of weeks ago before the dorms closed for the summer."

"Where are you living now?" Griff asked.

"I'm at my parents' house in Falmouth. I have a couple of classes to make up in the fall. I'll graduate in January."

"Okay to contact you there if we have more questions?"

"Do I have a choice?"

"One last thing," Griff said. "Did you ever notice anything odd about Ashley? Physically, I mean, like that she was shaky or jittery?"

Mitzi looked down as she dug the toe of her Adidas into the painted white line alongside the track. She shook her head and looked up at us, "No."

"Never?"

"She was stressed out all the time, anxious…yeah, but that was her norm."

We took Mitzi's contact information and with a nod to Coach Massett headed back toward the parking lot.

"What'd you think?" Griff asked.

"Don't have much more than we had before we got here. But it was interesting that Mitzi saw Gwen as more demanding than encouraging. It confirms what Dr. Varkin said about her needing Ashley to win in order to keep the family together."

"I don't think Ashley was aware of what was behind her mother's encouragement. She just saw smiles on her parents' faces. Greg came alive and Gwen was happy, and Ashley couldn't let them down. She won at any cost."

"Until it killed her."

"Yeah, until it killed her."

I slid onto the seat, warm from the sun coming through the windshield. Griff got in and closed the door. We sat in the parking lot watching the runners make laps on the track.

"You thinking she got into drugs to keep herself going?" I asked.

"I think it's a definite possibility. Poor kid never stood a chance."

"No shit," I said.

"You think Gwen was jealous of Ashley?"

"You mean because of her relationship with her father?"

"It's a thought."

I shook my head. "I don't think Gwen cares enough about Greg in that way. Like Carole said, she needs him for stability. I don't think love plays into it. And Greg loved Ashley's success, not his daughter. If you love your kid, you're not driving them into the ground to keep up a façade. What did Varkin call them?"

"A deeply disturbed family." Griff hit the button on the armrest and his window disappeared into the door. The breeze ruffled his hair and he slid his fingers through it. "People are messed up."

"Carole said Gwen was a good mother. I wonder if she felt responsible when Clayton died."

"You think she feels responsible for Ashley's suicide?"

"She hasn't said enough for me to know what she feels. But what parent doesn't question if there were things they could have done differently when they lose a child?"

"Clayton was sick. His death had nothing to do with her parenting."

"Everything about your children has to do with parenting. She probably thought she should have taken him to the doctor sooner or to a better doctor or to a more prestigious hospital. I think most mothers find ways to blame themselves when a catastrophe hits their kid and if they can't find a reason they create one."

Griff pushed the key into the ignition. The engine turned over. "Do you think Gwen places any blame with Greg?"

"Even if she does, she wouldn't voice it. It would be too risky. He's lost Clayton and Ashley, the two things that kept him home. She's got to come up with a new reason for him to stay. Blaming him would send him packing. If he's not considering it already."

"I think they're both to blame. I think they've been pushing her off that roof for years."

"A straight forward suicide?" I slipped a Honey Berry from my bag.

"Suicide, yes, straight forward, no." Griff reached over, slid the little cigar out of my fingers and into his coat pocket in one smooth move. "There's something about Mitzi's responses that don't ring true," he said, without missing a beat. "If Coach Massett noticed that Ashley was off, and he only saw her for a couple of hours a day, how could Mitzi not have noticed? They lived together. She'd have to have picked up on something."

I nodded. "Yeah, two girls living together are going to talk to each other, even if they aren't the best of friends. Even if it's just to be petty and argumentative, they'll talk. They can't not, it's a girl thing."

"See?" Griff said. "I know my feminine side."

TEN

We were scheduled to meet with lawyers at eleven-thirty. Since both parties were in a rush Peggy had worked some magic and slated an early closing on the house.

I'd come to my office first before heading to the bank and was sitting at my desk with the door shut, mentally prepping. After a second cup of coffee I pushed my mug aside. I was jittery enough. Not about moving in with Griff, we more or less lived together now at his place or mine. It was a sense of surrender that had my stomach cruising Space Mountain. How could I enjoy a Honey Berry without him giving me shit?

I took a deep breath and twirled a pen through my fingers. I loved him, no question there, but I was scared as hell to make the leap from self-sufficient to dependent. I know…it doesn't have to be that way. But isn't it built into the equation? One person equals dependent on self, two people equals dependent on each other. It took me years to find my own footing. A lot of it came with our last case. That tells you something about how long it's taken.

"Hey." Katie rapped her knuckles against my office door. "Time to get out of here and head to the closing. It's the big day."

Big day, I thought and tossed the pen aside. Huge day…the beginning of the end…or…the beginning of the beginning. It was my choice how to spin it.

I swung the door wide. "Put champagne on ice. We'll be back by noon."

"Done," Katie said and gave me a hug. She was privy to a few of my skeletons and left me to my own resolve this morning to work out the kinks. "One celebration coming up."

Griff had met with Peggy at the realty office early this morning to make sure everything was in order and insure a smooth closing. I pulled into the bank's parking lot and took the space beside his car. Hushing my stomach, I pulled the heavy glass door wide and stepped inside the building. The elevator rose to the third floor and when the doors parted I saw Griff looking out a window at the end of the hallway. As I walked toward him my confidence grew and so did my smile. The morning sun spilled over his face betraying a rushed shaving job (a little scruffy, just the way I like it). His hair was done in its usual coif. A quick shake of his head after stepping out of the shower, one swipe with the towel and voila, let it fall where it may. And like everything else about him, it worked. No hours of sweat at the gym and yet his body was as toned and hard as any twenty-something. Eyes that had witnessed hell, but still recognized beauty and a heart that had been broken once but was fearless and willing to try again.

He turned as I approached and reached a hand out for mine. "Ready?' he asked.

I nodded.

"Nervous?"

"No," I said smiling up at him and the funny thing was, I meant it.

We took seats on one side of the conference room table, across from a couple introduced by Peggy as the Morrows, the sellers of the property. And after a little more than an hour and with our hands sufficiently cramped from signing a mountain of forms in which we promised all but our first born, we were homeowners. We shook hands all around and then made our way to the elevators alongside the Morrows.

Peggy made small talk while we waited. "Talk about a small world, Mr. Cole's in the same line of business as Mike McKenzie."

Ellen Morrow's head shot up. Her eyes wide but guarded.

"Not exactly," Griff clarified. I'm a PI. On occasion my path crosses with the Portland PD, but more often I'm involved with the Criminal Investigation Unit. I don't know McKenzie directly."

I noticed Ellen squeeze her husband's hand.

"Sounds like Rhea will miss your daughter. Her name's Halsey, is that right?" I asked.

Mitch's jaw clenched, but he said nothing.

"They did get together occasionally," Ellen said. "But lately, not so much."

"Too bad. Must have been nice to have a babysitter that close by." I was hoping to provoke a longer response. From the look on Mitch's face there was some bad blood and I wanted to know more.

"You have children?" Mitch asked.

"No," I said.

He nodded. "You're lucky. Rhea seems to have a way of losing them."

"Mitch," Ellen scolded. "She didn't lose Halsey. She wandered off all by herself."

"That must have been scary," I prompted. The elevator bell signaled its arrival and the door in front of us parted. I stepped inside hoping she'd continue.

"We became a little leery about Halsey playing at McKenzie's after…," Ellen hesitated. "After Jonathan disappeared. He was a year old."

"Here one day, gone the next." Mitch snapped his fingers in front of my face. "I mean how does a one-year-old just disappear out of the house when his mother is home?"

"Mitch," Ellen said, her tone indicative of how many times she'd heard this before.

"Never found," he continued, "not even after a major manhunt. Mike being a cop the search went on for months, but they still found nothing. Who isn't going to be hesitant about their kid playing with that family? I mean Ellen and Rhea were friends. They were both pregnant at the same time, gave birth a month apart."

Ellen broke in. "After it first happened we didn't see Rhea at all. But after a year or so, after Halsey had turned two, Rhea was feeling better and started asking if she could come over and play. Offering to give us a night out. Halsey loved her, and I felt sorry for her, but I couldn't relax when they were together. Rhea's a nice person, but…"

"I never felt comfortable with Mike," Mitch interjected.

Ellen put her hand on her husband's arm. "Mitch."

"I don't care," he said. "They should know." He looked at Griff as though it was a guy thing. "There's something about him, you know?" I mean, how do you lose your kid out of your own house? Then one day Rhea comes running over and tells us Halsey had been in the back yard. She went inside to get them a snack and when she came out Halsey was gone." Mitch's voice was getting louder his anger mounting as he relived the moment.

"Mitch," Ellen said as the elevator doors opened.

She turned to Griff and me. "She'd just walked into the front yard gathering flowers. We found her within five minutes."

"But you can imagine what went through my head for those five minutes," Mitch said. "I wasn't being unreasonable. Anyway, after that I just couldn't allow Halsey to go to their house anymore."

Griff nodded. "I have a daughter. I get it."

"It all became very uncomfortable. When this job offer came up we grabbed the opportunity. Rhea means well, but I've always had the feeling that there's more going on in that house. Even before Jonathan was born something felt off."

"Okay Mitch, that's enough," Ellen said. "Look," she turned to me. "The McKenzies are solid people and they've had to deal with more than their share. I don't think Mike is a bad guy and they've been good neighbors. Who wouldn't be a little off after losing a kid, right?" She smiled. "I hope we haven't scared you. It's a great house. I'm sure you'll enjoy it."

Griff smiled and shook Mitch's hand. "Without a doubt, and good luck with your move."

Mitch looked at me, his eyes offering a warning he couldn't verbalize.

We watched them walk toward the parking lot. "Mitch doesn't mince words," I said.

"I can understand it. Most parents would feel the same way."

"But he acts like Rhea and Mike had something to do with Jonathan's disappearance. What parents would make their kid disappear?"

"There are some crazy parents out there."

"You don't need to tell me, but Rhea doesn't fit the profile of a psychotic parent. How much do you know about Mike?"

"Nothing about his personal life. He's a dedicated cop, and from what I hear, well liked."

"You asked John about him?"

Griff nodded.

John Stark is the head of CID, Portland's Criminal Investigation Unit and Griff's closest friend.

"Mike doesn't fit the psycho profile either."

I thought about the bruises I'd seen on Rhea but held my tongue. I needed proof before mentioning it to Griff. He hates assumptions.

"Anyway, how do we know it wasn't a real psycho who snuck in and took their kid? And now he's a million miles away from here?"

"We don't," I said. "Should we find out?"

"They already tried."

"But we haven't and we're the best there is."

"I won't disagree with that," Griff said. "But I don't think Rhea and Mike want to dig it all up again."

"Who says we tell them?"

"So we do it out of the goodness of our hearts? And behind their backs?"

"We do it for baby number two. Before he or she arrives it might be nice to know what happened to baby number one."

"I think we let sleeping dogs lie."

"How 'bout you let sleeping dogs lie and I wake them up?"

"If I disagree will you change your mind?"

"No."

"Then have at it, but keep it quiet, as in complete silence. I don't think Rhea or Mike would be pleased to find out you're investigating something I'm sure they're trying to put to rest."

"I'll bury my bones," I said. "No pun intended."

Eleven

We'd met with the moving company yesterday after the closing and refereed the packing at Griff's townhouse then the loading at my apartment. This morning the truck was stretched diagonally across the road as the driver inched forward and back, lining up the eighteen-wheeler with our narrow drive. Blocking traffic in both directions was a great way to introduce ourselves to the folks in North Yarmouth. Not that there were many cars at nine o'clock on a Saturday morning. A couple of produce laden pick-up trucks en route to the farmers market and a parent with a kid bouncing a soccer ball off the inside of the windshield. But first impressions matter.

Griff pulled the Land Rover into the driveway ahead of the truck and I followed in my Rav just as the trailer's back up signal began to sound. We parked alongside the house giving the truck ample space to position itself as close to the front porch as possible. Even though we'd opted to keep the Morrow's furniture and sent most of mine to a local consignment shop, we still had hours of lifting, pushing, pulling and carrying to keep us busy.

"I love it here," Allie said twirling around the driveway in little circles, her arms stretched wide. "It's so peaceful and private. I can sun bathe without the old man watching my every move."

"Who's that?" Griff asked.

"One of the men at Mom's condo. Every time I go to the pool he comes outside and sits on his porch. When I go in, he goes in. Talk about obvious."

"How old is he?" I asked.

"About a hundred," Allie laughed.

"He probably can't see much then," Griff said. "It's wishful thinking."

"Eeww, gross, Dad." Allie took off around the back of the house.

The driver slid the back door up along its rollers. His partner tossed a cigarette onto the front lawn. I held my tongue. By noon everything that had been inside the truck was inside the house in an anything goes arrangement. After a quick handshake, the guys got back into the truck, revved the engine and started down the drive. In that moment with just Allie and Griff and I standing in front of the house, no movers and no realtor, the house became home. I looked at Griff and from the smile on his face, knew he felt it too.

"Beer?" he said.

"In the plural."

"Champagne?" Allie came through the front door with an opened bottle of Gosset Grande Reserve Brut and three crystal glasses.

"Where'd you get that?" Griff asked.

"And these?" I lifted one of the crystal glasses from its precarious position on the narrow wooden rail.

"None of your business. Just drink and enjoy." She took the glass from my hand and set it once again on the porch railing and began to pour.

"You're not even old enough to buy let alone spend that much," Griff said.

"I have my connections."

"Allie."

"Okay, okay," she laughed. "It's a gift from Mom. She sends her congratulations. To *both* of you."

Eliza and I tolerate each other. She's a bit of a drama queen for me and I'm a little rough around the edges for her. But we make it work.

A cyclist was making their way down the dirt drive. We watched as Mike McKenzie approached.

"Now that's the way to move in." he said rolling to a stop in front of the porch steps. He was dressed in black, biking shorts and a yellow, reflective jersey.

"Wow, nice ride," Allie said eyeing the silver racing bike.

"Thanks. It's a Colnago, Italian made. Ever hear of Enzo Ferrari?"

"As in the sports car?" Griff asked.

"Yeah, the maker of these is connected to Ferrari. Racing bikes, racing cars, what more could any guy want?"

"I'll get another glass." Allie disappeared inside the house.

"So, today's the big day."

"Yeah," I said. "The day that ends with aching backs and ibuprofen."

Mike laughed and took the matching crystal champagne glass from Allie, holding it as she poured. "Well I have to say you folks know how to do things right." He lifted the glass in the air. "To good neighbors," he said.

We clinked our glasses together, the sun glinting off the crystal.

Griff nodded to his biking attire. "You just coming in or heading out?"

"Just back."

"You ride every day?"

"Every day I can. Rhea says it's an addiction," Mike laughed.

"Not a bad one to have. Ever do it professionally?" Griff asked.

"Used to, but now it's more of a hobby."

"Where is Rhea?" I asked.

"Napping. Those little rug rats have a way of wearing you out even before they're born." He smiled, tilting the champagne flute to his mouth. His knuckles were scraped and raw.

"Take a spill?" Griff asked nodding to his hand.

"No, more like had a fight, with a fifty-pound rock. We're redoing the landscaping around the pool. I'm putting in a stone wall." He looked at the back of his hand and shook his head. "Guess it got the best of me."

"That's why they have masons," I said.

"I know, but I hate to pay someone for a job I can do myself."

Like making a kid disappear, I thought. The accusation blew through my head before I could filter it. For three years in family law I'd witnessed the damage men could do to their wives and children, many of them upstanding citizens, judges, doctors…even cops.

Mike emptied his glass and set it on the railing. "I'll leave you folks to get settled in, but welcome and thanks for the drink."

"The first of many, I hope," Griff said. "Thanks for coming by."

With a wave, Mike disappeared into the trees.

"What does one of those bikes go for?" Griff asked Allie.

"I saw one in a biking magazine once for $17,000."

Griff glanced at me and raised his eyebrows.

"Cops must be doing pretty well these days."

"He seems nice." Allie took a sip of her champagne.

"They always do," I said.

"What's that supposed to mean?" Griff asked.

I shook my head. "Nothing…I don't know."

"People are innocent until proven guilty."

I realized that he was referring to the conversation we'd had about looking into Jonathan's disappearance, not the bruises I'd seen on Rhea.

I raised my glass. "To innocence," I said.

Twelve

"I was thinking I might pay Gwen a visit this morning," I told Griff as I dug through a cardboard box labeled *kitchen*. I unwrapped a couple of coffee mugs and set them on the counter. Crumpled newspaper fell to my feet.

"We should probably check in at the office first." Griff rummaged through another box and pulled out a bag of sugar.

"I was thinking I'd go alone."

He raised his eyebrows.

"I want to get clearer on her relationship with Ashley as well as how she feels about Greg and I think she might be more forthcoming if she's just talking to me. You know, woman to woman. No offense. I'm well aware of your therapeutic skills in drawing out information."

"Only when you're on a couch."

I pulled the frying pan from the box I was unpacking and gently conked him on the top of the head. "I'm trying to work here."

"All work and no play…"

"Christening our new bedroom last night wasn't enough for you?"

"I'm insatiable when you're around." He wrapped his arms around me. "And this is only the beginning. How does it feel?"

"Scary and wonderful," I said raising my face to his and kissing him.

"Get a room, you two." Allie stepped into the kitchen in gym shorts and a tee shirt. "What's for breakfast?"

Griff took the frying pan out of my grasp and handed it to Allie. "Whatever you want to make, but since all we have is one box of cereal and no milk you're limited."

She took the pan from his outstretched hand. "I can see my work is cut out for me."

"Yeah, and first off, timing is everything." He released me from his arms. "I'll shower and head for the office. You go see Gwen."

"What am I gonna do?" Allie asked.

Griff waved his arm at the sea of cardboard boxes. "Have at it."

I pulled into Lambert's driveway at ten o'clock relieved to see Greg's car was gone. Last time we were here he'd mentioned a standing tennis game on Wednesday mornings and I'd hoped that was still the case. Carole opened the door as I approached.

"Hi," she said with obvious surprise.

"I was hoping to talk with Gwen. Is she around?"

"In the garden. I'm on my way to the store, but c'mon in."

I followed her through the dank interior. Nothing had changed since our last visit. The place still felt like a catacomb. Unlike Gwen's garden, full of warmth and color and the scents of lilac and forsythia, I couldn't walk through the cold, dark interior fast enough. Carole pushed open the French doors and we stepped outside.

Gwen looked up, her face registering surprise. "Greg's not here," she said standing.

"Actually, I was hoping to speak with you."

She gestured to the wicker patio furniture. "Have a seat."

"You need anything before I go?" Carole asked.

Gwen looked at me and raised her eyebrows.

I shook my head. "No, I'm fine."

"I'll be back by lunchtime," Carole said and disappeared inside pulling the door closed behind her.

"What can I do for you, Ms. Callahan?"

"Britt," I said. "If it's not too difficult, I'd like to ask you about your relationship with Ashley."

She took a breath and looked past me out toward the pond and the ducks squawking and chasing after one another in the morning sun.

"Were you two close?" I asked.

"My daughter was everything to me. Both of my children were, but Clayton was Greg's. He was very possessive of his son from the moment he was born and so Ashley became more…mine, I guess."

"And you and Greg?"

Gwen's gaze had been resting on the ducks, but she looked at me now, her eyes narrowing. "What are you asking?"

"I'm sorry. I don't mean to be rude, but it will help a lot if I can get a sense of the family dynamics."

"Are you married?" she asked.

I shook my head. "No."

"People marry for many reasons. It's not always love that brings a man and a woman together."

"And what was it for you?"

She smiled. "You're persistent, aren't you?"

"So they say."

"Our families knew each other when we were children. We both had a country club upbringing if you know what I mean, lots of money and parties. Everything had to be perfect, though truth be told, it was all for show. It was my mother's way. She wasn't always the best mother, but to the world, she looked like she was and that's what mattered. I'm not ashamed to say that I've followed in her footsteps."

"Did your parents love each other?"

"Love? I have no idea. My father wasn't faithful, but he gave her what she needed, and I think that was enough for her."

"Carole told me you have a stepbrother. She said he wasn't welcome."

Gwen dismissed my comment with a wave of her hand. "Lowlife."

"Did you love your parents?"

"I had a string of nannies and babysitters. My parents took care of us, but never actually cared about us. I looked for love in other ways. I was eleven years old when I met Greg and by thirteen, I vowed that someday I would marry him. He was a few years older than me, and the leader of a pack of us kids who hung around the club unsupervised while our parents got sloppy in the bar. He took an interest in me and I did what I needed to in order to hold onto his interest."

"You're talking sexually?"

Gwen nodded.

"Didn't you say you were eleven when you met him?"

"Yes, and by the time I was thirteen we'd covered everything short of intercourse." She said it as casually as if she were disclosing what color paint she'd chosen for the living room.

"And Greg was how old?"

"He was eighteen when our relationship ended." Her eyes roamed my face watching for disapproval.

I held steady, no reaction. Who the hell was I to judge. If I'd been dating Griff at thirteen, he'd have been twenty-five.

"I grew up that summer," Gwen continued. "I was thirteen in June and twenty-five by August."

"And that's when the relationship ended?"

"Greg had been accepted at Yale. At the end of that summer both he and my father left."

"Your father left?"

"His new love interest was a waitress from the club. She was just ten years older than me."

"That must have been devastating."

"More for my mother. We were the talk of every cocktail party that year.

"Was this when your step-brother was born?"

"God no. That was years earlier. My father had some difficulty keeping it in his pants, as they say."

I suppressed a smile. Gwen did too.

"It was the norm for us," she continued. "My father came and went. But he always crawled back and like a fool my mother would open the door."

"Because she loved him?"

"Because she wanted the gossip to end and she wanted back in the club. In those days, there were no single parents on the country club scene. It was all his money. She didn't have a dime. We were nothing without him."

"Where's your father now?"

"I have no idea and I couldn't care less."

"But you and Greg kept in touch?"

"No, but I happened to run into him in the city one day. By that time, he'd graduated from Yale and was in his second year of law school. I was attending the University of Southern Maine. We began seeing each other. After he graduated we married."

"You were in love?"

She looked down at her hands and rubbed her thumb across her knuckles. "When Greg showed up in the bar that day, opportunity knocked. By marrying him I would gain back what I'd repeatedly lost during childhood."

"The Country Club?"

"Prestige. My children would know crystal and fine wines. They'd have Ivy League educations. And as long as he could be faithful or at least discreet, I would secure the appearance that my mother couldn't maintain."

"But did you love him?"

"For the first few years we jelled well enough, but after a while I could feel him becoming restless. Then we had Clayton."

"And?"

"He was obsessed with his son."

"And when Clayton died?"

"He couldn't bear to be in the house or around Ashley and me. I suggested that we move out of state, find a fresh start, but he told me that Clayton had been the only reason he'd stayed in the marriage. It was time for him to go."

"But he didn't."

She shook her head and looked out over her garden. "Ashley began showing so much promise in athletics that he started taking notice. I'd been attending her track events and school competitions all along, but Greg had seldom joined us. When she began winning, she piqued his interest. She was thrilled that he seemed happy again and was finally showing an interest in her."

"That must have put some pressure on her."

"You have no idea. Her anxiety went through the roof. She became terrified of losing a race, afraid he'd walk away if she wasn't consistently first in her class."

"Is that when she started seeing Dr. Varkin?"

"Yes, she'd seen him a few times after Clayton died to help her with the grief, but she started seeing him regularly as her success grew."

"And Greg stopped talking about leaving?"

"It never came up again." She looked back out over her garden. "I suppose it will now, though."

"And what about you? How did you feel knowing he was staying because of Ashley?"

"He was staying, that's all that mattered to me. My family was intact, as intact as it could be without Clayton."

"And where's your mother now?"

"Dead, finally. Suicide."

"I'm sorry."

"It's given Greg another reason to point his finger at me over Ashley's death. He says mental illness runs in my family. He said she got the genes to jump from me."

I hoped my face wasn't betraying the disgust I felt. Though Gwen didn't bat an eye.

"Do you think you and Greg will survive this? I mean, losing Ashley?"

She looked me dead in the eye. "I may have lived a life very similar to my mother's, but mine won't end as hers did. Greg's not going anywhere."

On my way back to the office, I thought about relationships and the random criteria people have for choosing a partner and keeping them. Money, prestige, loneliness, fear...what ever happened to love? Gwen honored ego over heart, like her mother. Mike and Rhea were harboring secrets. My gut said none of them were good. And both women were someone else entirely when their husbands weren't around. I had no doubt Greg and Gwen were going down, though she didn't know it yet. I had every hope Mike and Rhea would too. If honesty isn't the basis of a relationship, it can't weather the storms. I didn't know it as I drove back to the office, but clouds were gathering overhead. I just never saw them coming.

Thirteen

Griff eased the Rover through the State Street intersection in downtown Portland and took a right toward the west end. Gina Wellington had called. The toxicology report was in. The fact that she'd asked us to come to her office said it wasn't clean.

"I'm not feeling it," I said.

"Let's just wait and see what Gina has to tell us."

"Wait and see? That doesn't sound like you."

"It's Zen to be calm. Allie told me."

"I like you better as a hothead."

He raised his eyebrows.

We entered Gina's practice through her outer office door. It was lunchtime and the waiting room was empty.

"In here," she called and we followed the voice to her office.

She was sitting at her desk surrounded by neatly arranged stacks of paperwork. She caught me eyeing it.

"I try and play catch up during lunch, but today, it's not in the cards." She smiled, shoved a couple of stacks aside and motioned for us to sit down. "Thanks for coming. I assume you're still investigating Ashley Lambert's suicide?"

Griff nodded. "And?"

"Toxicology came back this morning."

"Anything out of the ordinary?"

"Before I answer, let me get the file. With two kids and a full time practice some days I can't remember my own name." Gina went to a gray metal file cabinet and pulled open the second drawer. She set the file on the desk and sat down. "Amphetamine," she said looking from Griff to me.

Specifically, Dextroamphetamine, the primary component in Adderall and Dexedrine."

"Aren't they similar?" I asked.

"Yeah, the Dexedrine is stronger, but it's a little odd that she was taking both unless she was using them at different times and for different things. I wasn't surprised to find Adderall. It was a trace amount. I mean I'd be hard pressed to find a college student at the end of the term who didn't have Adderall in their system." She gave a faint smile. "Given Ashley's life at the time with finals and graduation, that doesn't seem like a big deal. It certainly wasn't what killed her."

"What does an amphetamine do exactly?" I asked.

"They're primarily used for people with ADHD or narcolepsy. They promote wakefulness and focus, hence the appeal to college kids during finals. They're also used as appetite suppressants. Given Ashley's obsession with her weight, it makes sense. And amphetamine use increases energy, mental focus, stamina, confidence, the list goes on…"

"So they're attractive to athletes." Griff said.

"They are, but there are better things out there. I wouldn't consider amphetamines the drug of choice for professional athletes."

"What about nonprofessionals?"

"Possibly, I suppose if you're a college student, you're not really in the realm of the professional athlete, and things like Dexedrine and Adderall might be readily available on campus."

Griff shook his head. "Do you really think Ashley was into this? I mean, she was pursuing a Masters in Ethics. I can't see her going to these lengths no matter how pleased Greg was with her success."

"Science doesn't lie. She could have been using Adderall on a regular basis to decrease appetite and increase her academic focus. The Dexedrine could have provided an added boost on race days."

"How fast would they leave the body?"

Gina took a massive hardbound blue book from the shelf beside her desk. *Physician's Desk Reference* it said along the spine. She flipped through the pages until she'd found her answer. "That would depend on how often she took them, but in general they can be detected 12-24 hours after use with a standard blood test, longer with hair and urine."

"But if she was using either or both for racing and she hadn't had a race within the few days prior to her jump, neither one should have been in her system."

"That's the thing with any amphetamine. In the U.S. they're considered a Schedule II drug, which means highly addictive with a high potential for abuse. She may have started using solely for an athletic edge, but because of the addiction factor, it became hard for her to stop. A lot of people think they'll just use an amphetamine for quick weight loss or during finals week and before they know it they're serial users."

"Coach Massett said the NCAA did random drug tests at races. Wouldn't it have been picked up?"

"Not necessarily. If she was injecting, the drug's response rate is immediate. She could have done the test then hit the locker room right before the race for an injection and if she'd laid off of it for a few days prior to the race, then she'd test clean."

"Jesus," I said. "That seems crazy."

"Crazy, but doable," Gina said. "If she had her timing down. It would have been out of her body before the test and then she injects it just before race time."

"But you didn't find injection sights on autopsy, did you?"

Gina shook her head. "No, but drugs were not in question at that time and due to the condition of her body, let's just say any injection site would have been close to impossible to find. Amphetamines can be swallowed, snorted, smoked and mixed with water to take intravenously. My guess is she was shooting it, because the timing would be right, but I could be wrong. Regardless, the fact remains that it was getting into her somehow. For Ashley, it would have been a miracle drug. It increased her physical activity, kept her alert and awake, and provided a sense of confidence. While it was doing all that to enhance her running, it also increased the Dopamine in her brain giving her a sense of euphoria. It must have felt like a little piece of heaven, given the stress she was under."

"And long-term effects?"

"Anxiety, confusion, insomnia, motor excitation, poor balance, psychosis…I can keep going."

"That everything?" Griff asked.

"Isn't that enough?" I said.

"Not exactly." Gina let out a sigh. "There is one other thing, but it's practically impossible to prove."

I groaned.

"What's that?" Griff asked.

"Erythropoietin or EPO, a protein hormone produced by the kidneys. Released into the blood stream, it binds with receptors in bone marrow and stimulates the production of red blood cells. A performance enhancer."

"Since my performance is already extraordinary," Griff looked at me and winked. "I'm not well versed in enhancers. How does EPO provide an edge?"

I rolled my eyes and caught the smirk on Gina's face before she got serious again and answered. "Red blood cells carry oxygen, so the more RBCs in your body the more oxygen you have, which increases stamina and endurance. An athlete will give themselves an injection right before a race."

"Seems a little out of Ashley's league," Griff said.

"I would have said the same thing about amphetamines until the tox screen came back," Gina said.

"Did this EPO stuff show up?"

"It's not that easy. The way it was originally detected or more accurately, suspected, is when an athlete's hematocrit level was too high, over 50%. Now there's an accurate urine test, but we only have Ashley's blood to work with."

"And?"

"Her hematocrit was well over 50%, making me suspect EPO in her system. It's something else to think about."

"Like you haven't given us enough," I said. "She would have had to inject right before a race. That would mean her time and privacy were limited. Could she have mixed the two? Like a syringe full of EPO and Dexedrine? A two for the price of one injection?"

"I don't see why not."

We thanked Gina and stepped out onto the sidewalk.

"Talk about not knowing someone." He checked his watch. "It's almost six o'clock. Better head home and see how far Allie's come with the unpacking."

"Not before some fortification. After hearing all that from Gina, I need to process with a glass of wine…maybe two. And there's no food at the house. We can get take-out for Allie."

"Twist my arm," Griff said.

At Gritty's Brew Pub, we seated ourselves at a table on the deck. Within minutes the waiter set a Black Fly Stout and a Pinot Grigio in front of us. It's good to be known. Gritty's is our other stomping ground. Where Conundrum is a skirt and heels, Gritty's is shorts and flip-flops. It depends on our mood.

"So?" Griff said, taking a drink.

"Hard to believe."

"Coach did say she seemed a little high strung lately, talking incessantly. I think he called it, rambling."

"Yeah, but that wouldn't make one think drugs."

"Mitzi said she'd seemed anxious and didn't sleep."

"Again, neither screams drugs. It's like Dr. Varkin said. If she was using, it was buried so deep no one knew."

"I keep thinking about Carole saying, she was too good," Griff said. "Miles ahead of the competition. I guess now we know why."

"Where was she getting it? Dr. Varkin said he'd never prescribed anything for her."

"We need to ask Greg who her family doctor was."

"But they wouldn't have been giving her EPO. That's the trail we need to follow. She could have gotten Adderall or Dexedrine on campus, but EPO is in a different league altogether." I took a long swallow and motioned for the waiter.

"How the hell are we going to deliver this news to Greg Lambert?"

"Very carefully. But, hey, he's human. He's gotta know everyone's got secrets."

"You keeping anything from me?" Griff asked.

I thought about what I hadn't told him regarding Mike McKenzie, but that was still a suspicion. "I've told you all there is to know about me."

"Let's keep it that way," he said.

We raised our glasses and toasted the promise. What I didn't know then, was how tough that promise would be to keep.

Fourteen

Allie surprised us with a box-free kitchen. Everything was put away and organized.

"Ahh, payment," she said lifting the take-out containers we'd brought from Gritty's from my arms.

"Looks great." Griff walked around the kitchen opening and closing cabinets. "Must have taken you all day."

"Almost, except for when Rhea McKenzie came over."

"What did she want?" I asked between spoonfuls of chili.

"She stopped by to say hello and see how the move was going. She brought a lemon pound cake." Allie pointed to a small square of tin foil on the counter.

Griff picked it up peeling the tin foil back. "This all of it? Looks more like a cupcake."

"It was the only food in the house. I ate it for lunch and again later for a snack."

Griff raised his eyebrows and bounced the ball of tin foil in the palm of his hand.

"What? I was hungry. I've been working hard putting your kitchen together."

He laughed and dropped the foil ball on the counter. "Guess I forgot about groceries. Take care of that first thing tomorrow."

"What else did Rhea have to say?" I asked.

"Not much, but she was on crutches. Sprained her ankle. Must suck to be on crutches when you're pregnant."

"What happened?"

"Said she slipped on the stairs."

"I'll go over in the morning and thank her. If we're going to the market maybe I can pick up a few things for her." I knew when I asked about the crutches Rhea would give me another inadequate explanation just as she had about the bruises. And we'd both known she was lying.

"It's her left one," Allie continued. "She can probably still drive. Unless she has a stick shift."

"She had a couple of bruises on her back last time I saw her. She said she'd slipped then too."

"Sounds like our neighbor's a little accident prone," Griff said.

"Or not," I said.

He looked at me. "What are you implying?"

"Nothing yet, but I'm keeping my options open. I'm not convinced that she slipped. Not all of the bruises I saw were fresh. She'd have to have slipped numerous times over the past few weeks for her back to look the way it did."

Griff didn't say anything. He just looked at me.

"I've never heard a bad thing about Mike," he said.

"Like I said I'm not jumping to conclusions, just keeping an open mind. But don't forget, they don't all look like scumbags. They can be wearing a blue uniform just as easily as a hoodie or a wife beater."

"I know that, but he's really well liked on the force."

I nodded. "All the more reason to befriend Rhea. If my gut's right who the hell else does she have?"

"Don't get in the middle of it, Britt. There are places she can go for help if she wants it. You're not in that line of work anymore and if you're right and that's what's happening it'll be a shit show if it comes out. I'm not saying don't be her friend, just give her the resources she needs. Don't get into the thick of it yourself."

"That doesn't sound like you."

"Look, if she tells you he's abusive there's nothing I won't do to help her. You know that. I'm just saying if you move forward on an assumption and you're wrong, you could damage a lot of careers, your own included."

I looked at him and nodded. But I didn't say I wouldn't get in the thick of it because that's exactly where I knew I'd be if she confided in me. I never stay at arms- length in anything I do. And I'm not about to start now.

The next morning after brewing a pot of coffee I settled myself in the master bathroom with a full mug and eight cardboard boxes. Griff was still asleep. I sat on the tub and surveyed my mission. I was thrilled with our new house, loved every inch of it, but the chore of settling in and making it a home was not my strong suit. I know women are supposed to love nesting. It's an innate part of being female, but I missed that chromosome. Blame my mother. (I like to blame her for most things.) She didn't know a sauté pan from a bedpan. The homemaking gene, dominant in my sister Amy, lies dormant in me. Amy can cook a gourmet meal in a kitchen off the cover of House Beautiful. I bring home take-out and make a mean martini. (Thanks, Mom.)

"You look busy."

I looked up from my perch on the edge of the bathtub and nodded at the stacks of boxes. "I'm working out a game plan in my head."

"Oh," Griff said. "Like how to get out of unpacking?"

"Exactly, and now that you're awake I have my means of escape." I set my coffee on the sink and put my palms on his chest gently nudging him backward into the bedroom until his knees buckled at the edge of the bed.

"I like your plan, Callahan. It's a definite game changer." He laid back across our king size mattress and pulled me over him like a blanket.

Afterward…in my search for shampoo and body wash, I managed to empty one of the boxes and my plan fell into place. As I searched for things the boxes would virtually unpack themselves and I'd be done in a week. Griff wouldn't care how long it took because…well…he's a man.

"Ready for the market?" he called from downstairs.

"Yeah, just let me run over to Rhea's first and see if she needs anything."

"I know what you're doing," he said.

"What?"

"Snooping."

"I am not. I'm being a good neighbor." I walked past him and out the back door.

"You are so," he yelled after me.

"Whatever," I said under my breath pushing branches out of my way as I took the path between our houses.

Rhea was stretched on a chaise beside the pool, her face tipped to the sun. She was a small woman, thin other than her baby bump and short, her feet barely reaching the end of the chair. Her unruly hair was twisted into a bun at the nape of her neck. A few chestnut strands whipped about her head in the breeze.

"Hi," I said.

She sat straight up, her feet hitting the concrete. "Oh my God, Britt," she said, hand on her chest. "You scared me."

"I'm sorry. I didn't mean to startle you. Allie mentioned you were on crutches. We're headed to the market. I thought I could get some things for you if you need me to."

"That's really kind of you, but I sent Mike off to work this morning with a grocery list. He'll take care of it. Oh, but..."

"You forgot something."

"Ice cream. I'm having a craving for pistachio."

"Consider it done."

"Only if you'll stay and have some with me when you get back."

"Count on it," I said and turned back to the path. On my way to the house I congratulated myself on how I'd handled our interaction. If I'd made too much of her ankle right off the bat, she'd have put her guard up. What better way to ease into it than over a bowl of pistachio ice cream? My interrogation skills were getting better all the time. Not that I was going to flat out interrogate Rhea. But in truth, I was after more than friendship.

"I assume you're taking the day off," Griff said as he pulled into McKenzie's driveway, dropping me off with a half-gallon of ice cream.

"You're going to the office?"

"I'll drop this stuff home first," he nodded toward the groceries in the back seat, "and head in."

"You don't mind?"

"Somebody's got to pay the mortgage."

I kissed him on the cheek and closed the Land Rover's door. I didn't tell him I considered myself to be on a case. He'd told me to keep my nose out of it and I would. It was my mouth that would be doing the work.

Rhea was still stretched on the chaise when I stepped through the chain link fence that surrounded the pool. "Don't get up," I said raising an outstretched arm. "I'm sure I can find a couple of bowls and spoons. I'm a PI, remember?"

She laughed and settled back onto the lounge tipping her face to the sun.

Inside the house, I glanced around, opened a few drawers and flipped through a stack of mail sitting on the counter. The kitchen flowed down two steps into a family room. A fireplace faced me, a flat-screen television mounted on the wall above it. An over-sized, black leather sectional and a baby grand piano finished of the room. Nice spread for a cop's salary. A staircase beyond led to the second floor. Too risky for now, but an office on the other side of the family room lured me in. The Police Academy diploma and certifications hanging in black metal frames told me it was Mike's office. I always find hanging your diploma in your home a bit egotistical. Your place of employment is one thing. Clients need to know you have a brain before they lay out their cash or write a check, but at home? It's a little much.

"Britt?"

"Shit." Rhea was in the kitchen. "Hi," I said hurrying back through the family room toward her. "I couldn't help myself. Your home is beautiful. I just took a quick peek. Hope that's okay."

She looked at me and tried to smile, but her mouth wouldn't cooperate.

"I'm sorry," I said. "I didn't mean to overstep my welcome."

That seemed to appease her and the smile appeared. "No worries," she said and opened a drawer to her right taking out two spoons.

"Bowls?" I asked.

"Over there." She pointed to an overhead cabinet.

Equipped with the necessary tools we settled poolside and filled our bowls with green ice cream laden with pistachio nuts.

"How's the ankle?" I asked between spoonfuls.

"Better today, but it hurt like hell when it happened."

"What did you do again? Allie told me, but my memory is selective."

Rhea laughed and I felt like I was back on her good side.

"Nothing really, I just missed a step coming down the stairs. I was carrying a basket of laundry. Between my stomach and the basket, I couldn't see what my feet were doing."

"That'll teach you to do laundry. Maybe Mike ought to pick up that chore for now."

"Oh right." She grinned. "A cop doing housework? Like that'll happen."

"He's one of those?"

"To the core. He works outside the house. I work inside. The two never overlap."

"Not even when you're pregnant?"

She shook her head and sucked a mound of green into her mouth. "I don't mind. We decided when we got married that I'd raise the kids and care for the house and he'd bring home the paycheck. I think he'd feel insulted if I wanted to work," she added. "Even now that we…even since…" She let the words trail off.

We were quiet for a few beats, licking our spoons.

"You must be excited about the new baby," I said hoping to dispel the weight that had fallen on the conversation. But, she didn't answer and I noticed her eyes fill. Way to go, Britt. "I'm sorry," I said. (I'd lost track of how many times I'd felt the need to apologize since I'd arrived.) "I didn't mean to bring up…"

She shook her head and sniffed. "No, it's okay. I'm just hoping for an easy delivery. I haven't looked past that."

"How much longer do you have?" I asked.

"Three and a half weeks."

"Nursery ready?"

She set her bowl on the glass tabletop between us. "No. I haven't made a nursery. We have a guest room. I put a bassinet in there. It's really all you need in the beginning."

It was one of those rare moments when I had no words. What parents put their new baby in a guest room, like it's going to be with them for a limited amount of time? Jonathan came to mind. ("How does a one-year-old just disappear out of his house with his mother home?") Then again, maybe the fear of something awful happening again kept Rhea from creating a nursery. Maybe it was just too reminiscent, too painful. Putting their little bundle of joy in the guest room could be understandable, strange, but understandable, right? Yeah, but no. The discomfort between us was palpable.

"Thanks for coming over, Britt," she said, "and for the ice cream."

Relieved, I took my cue to leave. "You're welcome. Let me know if there's anything else you need." I reached for the bowls. "I'll take these in."

"Just leave them in the sink," she said. "It'll give me something to do when I go inside."

After depositing the bowls, I came down the stone stairway and started to walk away, but hesitated conscious of the elephant in the room. I turned back. "Rhea, are you okay?"

She looked at me a long moment before answering and then very slowly nodded her head, still holding onto my eyes. "I manage," she said.

Something passed between us. I wasn't sure what, but my grandmother would have called it a 'knowing'.

Fifteen

The next morning it was back to work for me. No more lounging poolside with pistachio ice cream. In my mind I'd been gathering evidence, but to Griff, I'd taken the day off. After visiting with Rhea, I'd driven Allie home relieving her of more unpacking. On a whim, I'd picked up Chardonnay, steamers, potatoes and corn on the cob. A traditional New England Clam Bake complete with Death by Chocolate for dessert. If Griff had been irritated by my playing hooky, it was forgotten the minute he came through the door.

But this morning we were back in the swing and on our way to the office via the back road from Yarmouth to Portland. Route 9 is mostly pasture. Horses munched their breakfast, tossed away flies with a shake of their head and rolled in the dirt scratching their backs. Like them, we were enjoying a slow start to a lazy summer day.

"Pretty," I said gazing out the window of the Land Rover.

"Be prettier without that," Griff said pointing to a clearing where bulldozers and dump trucks waited, their engines running. "Looks like a new development going in."

"Why can't they ever just leave land untouched?"

"Money."

I shook my head. "Every house looks the same."

Griff took a sip of his coffee.

"What's that huge hole?"

Off to one side, away from the paved road that led to the houses was a hole in the earth at least twelve feet deep, the length and width of an extremely large house.

"Pool? Don't know what else it could be."

"Nice. A community pool."

"As in gated community," he said, pointing to the sign we were passing.

Royal Oaks

(A Gated Community)

"Why's gated community in parenthesis?"
"Less arrogant."
"Guess we'll have to get our own pool," I said.
"With you and Allie on my back it'll be sooner than later."
"Squeaky wheel."
He smiled. "Or maybe it's because I love my girls."
"You always manage to come out on top."
"Just the way I like it."

"It's about time, you two," Katie said as we came through the door.

I handed her a bag from Dick's doughnuts, her favorite.

"Bribery will get you everywhere," she said taking a bear claw from the bag and closing her eyes as she took a bite. "Mmm, heaven. There's a stack of mail on each of your desks and phone messages. Nothing crazy or I would have called. How's the house?"

"Full of boxes," I said. "You like unpacking?"

"Wish I could, but someone's gotta take care of things here." She smiled and chewed.

"Likely excuse," I said and stepped into my office.

By noon emails and phone calls had been returned and a meeting for a new case scheduled. Cheating spouse. I hated those. There was never a good outcome for anyone except our bank account and even though that would make the pool close enough to touch, it never felt good depositing a check that had been written through tears.

"What about paying Mitzi another visit?" Griff said from the doorway.

"You know where she lives?"

He looked at me, confused. "I'm a PI. What do you think?"

I laughed. "Lighten up. I wasn't insulting your ability. You think she's got something?"

He shrugged. "She lived with Ashley for the past year. Even if they weren't the best of friends, you learn a lot about someone when you live with them."

"Is that a warning?"

"What're you, paranoid, Callahan?"

I looked at him from behind my desk and tipped my head, a smile played around the edges of my mouth. "No." My voice was just above a whisper. My plan to walk knee deep through Rhea's life felt less dishonest that way.

Falmouth is one of the wealthiest communities in the state and its residents like to keep it that way. They stand elbow to elbow leaving no space for intruders. Whether they're sipping Starbucks on the sideline at their kids' soccer game or martinis at The Woodlands, the exclusive country club that chooses its members like a chef chooses tomatoes, they don't make room for commoners. But every family has its Uncle Buck. They're inescapable. Those folks that live on the outskirts of town rather than butt to shoreline, where kids wear sneakers out of boxes that say Target instead of Under Armour. And that's where Mitzi's address of 297 Western Ave. took us.

We pulled into the driveway of a brown ranch. A wooden wagon wheel leaned against a fir tree with the numbers 2 and 7 nailed into two spokes. We guessed the empty spindle between them was where the 9 should have been. A statue of Saint Francis stood in front of the wheel. Above it, a birdfeeder swung in the breeze.

"Help you?" A man in his fifties wearing a navy blue, net tank top and camouflage shorts stepped out of the darkened garage squinting in the sunlight. He held a greasy rag in one hand and ran it over the back of his neck while swatting at a fly with the other.

"We're looking for Mitzi Gannon," Griff said. "She live here?"

"Who are you?"

"Griff Cole." He reached a hand toward the man who stepped forward and shook it. With the other hand, Griff offered his ID.

"I'm Gary Gannon, Mitzi's father." He glanced at the ID then looked at the oil on his palm and wiped it with the rag in his hand. "Sorry, workin' on the beater." He nodded over his shoulder toward a rusty blue F-150 in the garage. Thing never makes it through more than two or three months without shittin' the bed. See you got one yourself." He nodded towards Griff's Land Rover.

"Oh no," Griff laughed. "She's in pristine condition. They don't make 'em like that one anymore. She's a Series III, 1975. Smooth as a twelve-year-old single malt."

I turned my head so Griff wouldn't see my eyes roll.

"Don't kid yourself. They all go one day. 1975 was forty years ago, you better hit your knees if you're thinkin' she'll last much longer."

I knew this was cutting straight to the heart so I stepped in to ease Griff's pain. "Hi," I said reaching for Gary's hand. "I'm Britt Callahan, we're private investigators looking into the death of Ashley Lambert. I understand Mitzi was Ashley's roommate."

Gary shook his head. "Terrible thing. Kid had everything going for her. Don't make sense."

"That's how her parents feel," I said. "We're trying to get them some answers. Is Mitzi home?"

"Believe so...Mitzi." He let out a bellow that could challenge a foghorn. "Kid's probably got them ear plugs glued to her head." He moved toward the house and motioned for us to follow.

We passed the traditional Mary-on-the-half shell, surrounded by a garden desperate for a good weeding. After Mary came three little angels each holding a black metal lantern that when lit, would guide a visitor up the flagstone walkway. A two-foot crucifix made of grapevines and backed by dried up, pine boughs hung beside the back door. We stepped into a kitchen that looked more like some kind of do-it-yourself chapel. At least a dozen stained glass sun catchers hung in the bay window behind the sink, splashing color over every surface in the small room. Most of them were angels, a few crosses and two doves. The walls took up where the window left off with pictures of Jesus from childhood through adulthood culminating with the three crosses on the Mount. There were shelves of religious figurines and small crystal dishes of water, holy I'm sure, strategically placed at each doorway so you could bless yourself coming and going. I was sure Griff was as overtaken by the place as I was because neither of us spoke. Finally, my eyes fell on normalcy, a stack of mail on the kitchen table next to a plate with a smattering of dried egg yolk and a mug half full of coffee.

"The wife works nights," Gary said following my gaze.

I assumed that was his way of explaining why there was also a pile of dishes in the sink. I wondered how Gary could fix a car but wasn't able to wash a dish. Must have a problem with soap and a sponge.

"Mitzi?" Gary yelled up the stairway.

"Yeah?"

"Someone to see you."

"Have a seat. She'll be right down." He picked up the plate and mug from the table and balanced them on top of the already overflowing sink. "I gotta get back to work." He stepped outside letting the screen door slam behind him.

"I knew I'd see you again." Mitzi came into the kitchen, slid a wooden captain's chair across the linoleum and sat.

"We have a few more questions," Griff said.

"Shoot." She picked up a spoon from the table and tapped it against the palm of her other hand.

"Was there any reason for you to think Ashley might have been using drugs?"

She shrugged and shook her head. "No. I mean, not really. I saw some Adderall in her bag once. I was a little surprised that perfect Ashley would stoop the way the rest of us did at exam time, but I was kinda glad too, it made her seem more normal."

"Ever see anything else out of the ordinary?"

"You mean in the way of drugs?"

I nodded.

"She wasn't the type."

"You think it was normal for her to be as good as she was?" I asked. "I mean she never lost, right? What are the odds of that?"

"Some people are good at what they do."

"How are your races going?" Griff asked.

She looked at him like she wasn't sure how to answer.

"Coach Massett said you were his number two finisher. Said you couldn't get past Ashley. Must be nice not to be second anymore."

"What are you saying?" she asked.

"I'm not saying anything. I'm asking you how your running is going."

"It's going fine."

"First place finishes?"

She nodded without taking her eyes off Griff.

"Congratulations."

"Did Ashley have a lot of money?" I asked changing the subject hoping to drop her intensity down a notch.

She broke her stare with Griff, tossed the spoon onto the table and shifted to me, but the muscles in her face didn't relax. "Why?"

"I'm just trying to get a sense of her lifestyle away from her parents. Did they give her an allowance? Did she work part time?"

"She had a bank account and a checkbook and credit cards. She didn't work. Somebody kept her in money and paid her bills."

"So, she had plenty?"

"I looked at her checkbook once when she was in the shower. She left it lying on the bed. There was a five-figure balance and the first number was 5. That should give you an idea."

"Not bad for a college student," I said.

Mitzi scoffed. "No shit."

"But no drugs as far as you know?"

"You're talking to me like I knew her well. I didn't know crap about her except that she was a spoiled rich girl with an overbearing mother and a father who wouldn't stay on the sideline."

Griff stood. "Thanks for your help Mitzi." He pushed his chair back beneath the wooden table. "There is something I've been wondering. I hope I'm not out of line by asking, but Fensworth is a very expensive school. I was wondering…"

"How a lowlife like me got in?" Mitzi finished his sentence.

"That wasn't quite how I'd put it."

"Yeah, but it's what you're wondering."

Griff waited.

"I got a full scholarship. Athletic and academic."

"That must have made it even harder for you to witness Ashley's success."

"I'm getting my education. That's what I'm there for. And this year I'll own the track. I'm doin' just fine, thank you."

"I hope so," Griff said.

I followed Griff outside. Behind me Mitzi's chair scraped across the floor and the door closed.

Griff leaned his head into the garage. "Nice to meet you Gary," he said.

"Likewise." Mr. Gannon stood up from under the hood of the pick-up and wiped his hand on the rag he took from his pocket.

Griff stuffed his hands into his jeans. "It must have been tough for you to watch your daughter work so hard just to come up second every time."

Gary Gannon took a deep breath stretching his torso an inch or two taller. "The Proverbs say, *Pride goes before destruction and a haughty spirit before a fall. But with the humble is wisdom.* We have the Lord on our side. Obviously, Ashley Lambert didn't. She took the fall. Those are God's words."

For the second time since we'd arrived at the Gannon's house we had no response. Griff nodded to Gary, put a hand on my shoulder and turned me toward the Land Rover.

"Jesus," I said as we backed out of the driveway.

"You invoking or swearing?" Griff asked.

"A little of both."

"Quite the family. I don't really know how to describe them."

"Sort of like Evangelical Bundys."

Griff laughed. "I think you hit the nail on the head."

"Or the thorns."

"Don't start, Britt. You could get struck down."

"Nah, I think He likes me."

"He'd be a fool not to."

Sixteen

"You up for a visit with Greg Lambert?" Griff asked as we started across the Casco Bay Bridge.

"You're ready to disclose Ashley's drug use?"

"Not yet."

"What if Gina called him?"

"I asked her to give me a couple of days."

"What are we seeing him for?"

"Greg must know about her finances. He's probably controlling them. If we can access her money flow we can see where she was spending it."

"Leading us to who she was buying from." I said.

"Exactly."

"You still think it was suicide?"

"Yeah, but the drugs are a curve ball. Before we lay it out for Gwen and Greg I want to make sure we can back up what we tell them with solid proof."

Greg Lambert never looked happy to see us and his greeting today was no different.

"What?" he asked swinging wide the front door.

"Nice to see you too, Greg," Griff panned. "We need a little insight regarding Ashley's financial situation."

"Like what?"

"I'm assuming you supported her. She wasn't working, correct?"

Greg gestured for us to come inside. We followed him into his study. He stopped and turned to us mid-way across the plush carpet. No offer to sit down.

"What are you getting at?"

"I'm developing a bit of a theory and need to know how Ashley spent her money."

"What's your theory?'

"I'd rather not get into it yet, not until I know if I'm right."

"I hired you, Mr. Cole, at a hefty price I might add. I have a right to know your theories."

Griff nodded. "That's true, but you might not like where I'm going."

"I'll decide what I like and don't like."

"All right. Ashley was good, almost too good. I mean most kids have it one way or another. They're off the charts academically or athletically, but both is less common."

"So? My daughter was gifted."

"Gifted or assisted."

"What the hell does that mean?"

"Is it possible Ashley was using performance enhancers to win her races?"

"Perform…what the hell? Are you telling me she was taking drugs?"

"The toxicity screen came back. Ashley had amphetamines in her system."

Greg stood there staring at Griff, processing the information. He was in fight or flight mode and I was pretty sure which way Greg would go."

"That's bullshit."

I was right.

"I asked Dr. Wellington to give me a couple of days to look into it, but you can call her to confirm." Griff nodded toward the phone on the desk.

"You're damn right I'll call her to confirm."

Greg picked up his cell phone and punched in a few numbers. After a brief conversation with Gina he put the phone carefully on the desk, stared at it for a moment like he thought it might change its mind and then slowly turned to face us.

"What is it that you want to know?"

His tone had softened, become almost repentant. (Almost.).

"I'd like to know how she spent her money."

Greg Lambert didn't move other than to clench and unclench his fists while he stared at the floor in his study.

"I'm hoping that might tell us how and where she was getting the drugs."

"They tested her once in a while at a meet," Greg said. "She always tested clean."

"Professional athletes get around drug testing all the time."

Greg's head shot up and he leveled his eyes at Griff. "Professional..." He stopped.

"Something you want to say?" Griff asked. "If you know something that will help...."

"I don't know anything,"

Griff shrugged, "It's your dime."

"Ashley had a bank account and a checkbook. I paid her credit card bills. She was very careful. I never saw anything out of the ordinary on the statements."

"What about her checking account?" I asked. "Was she the only name on the account?"

He nodded. "She used that for personal things. I deposited five thousand a month. She seemed content with that amount."

Who wouldn't be, I thought. A brilliant kid and stellar athlete heading for Johns Hopkins with money in the bank takes drugs and jumps to her death. WTF?

"Can we take a look at her bank statements?" Griff asked.

"I don't have them. They went directly to her. I have no idea what she did with them."

"But the bank would have copies. Or we could access them from her computer."

Greg waved his hand in the air. "I'm her executor, but I don't have any of her passwords. You're better off going to the bank directly."

Will you give us permission to request her statements?"

"I'll call the manager. He knows me. When do you want them?"

Griff raised his eyebrows. "How about now?"

Greg Lambert picked up the phone and made the arrangements and Griff and I headed to Citizens Bank in downtown Portland.

Bank Manager Steven Connelly stood and shook Griff's hand after we introduced ourselves.

"I have them right here. I printed everything immediately after Mr. Lambert made the request."

Money talks, I thought and right now we were hoping it would talk in more ways than one.

Griff took the envelope from Mr. Connelly and after a quick stop at *Silly's* for fish tacos, we were on our way back to the office to study Ashley's spending habits.

We were two blocks from downtown when we stopped for a red light. On the corner to my left was a Mobil station, to my right, The Blue Kangaroo Day Care. Kids of working parents ranging in age from two to eight were playing inside the fenced yard. The light changed and we started to pull away. It was then that I noticed a short, pregnant woman standing at the far corner of the fenced play yard. Her unruly hair whipped about her face in the summer breeze, but there was no mistaking her features. It was Rhea standing in the shade of the Maple tree, almost unseen in its shadow, watching the children play. My first thought was how sad she looked, her shoulders stooped, her hands folded together as if in prayer. I wondered if she was imagining Jonathan on that playground. Then I wondered if she was watching the children in anticipation of her own child and the hopes and fantasies that must accompany an approaching birth. I wanted to believe it was the latter, but my gut knew better. I turned my head as we pulled forward so I could keep watching her.

"What are you looking at?" Griff asked.

"It's Rhea. She's standing at the day care watching the kids."

"So?"

"This far from home? At a day care? What's she doing?"

"Maybe scoping it out for the baby."

"She's a stay at home Mom. She told me that's the way she and Mike want it. He works outside the home. She works in."

"Maybe she wants a day off once in a while."

"Yeah," I said and settled back in the seat. "Maybe."

"Any calls?" Griff asked over his shoulder as we crossed the threshold into his office, anxious to get to Ashley's bank statements.

"Greg Lambert," Katie said following us in.

"We were just there."

"He wanted to know if you'd found anything."

Griff shook his head and grimaced. "He'll know when I do."

"Should I tell him that?"

"Yes."

She smiled and pulled the door closed.

Griff handed me a stack of statements that started with the opening of the account and ended two years ago. He took the more recent ones. It didn't take long to see a glaring change in Ashley's spending pattern. The statements I had were boring, run of the mill purchases, doctor appointment co-pays, Varkin was listed almost monthly, CVS, Amazon orders. All in all, nothing out of the ordinary, but Griff's stack revealed something different. As of last year, on the first of every month, eight thousand dollars had been withdrawn in cash. The five-figure balance that Mitzi had mentioned was long gone. From the looks of it Ashley was just scraping by. Greg hadn't made any mention regarding changing the amount he deposited monthly. And in fact, it was clear to see a five-thousand-dollar deposit was made on the first of each month. But with an eight-thousand-dollar withdrawal the day after, Ashley's funds were close to depleted.

"What do you think?" Griff asked.

"No idea. Even if she was buying performance drugs they wouldn't have run her $8000 a month, would they?"

"Seems doubtful, but I guess that's our next direction."

"Drugs?"

"Performance enhancers."

"How do you find people who will talk about that? Isn't that whole faction pretty secretive?"

"I don't know. It's all new to me. But someone might be willing to offer advice to a newbie online. It'll be anonymous. No risk."

"Everyone likes to give advice."

"Play to the ego."

Seventeen

I'd collapsed onto a lounge out on the deck after completing a half hour on the elliptical. My skin was sticky with half dried sweat. I was imagining the pool that would someday grace the stretch of lawn before me and wishing it were there now. Griff had left for the office after his last swallow of caffeine to further research PE use. I'd begged off an early start in favor of a workout and told him I'd join him later, leaving out my plan to drop in on Rhea next door. Hey, who could fault me for checking in on a pregnant woman with a sprained ankle? Who, other than Griff that is. Seeing Rhea standing by the day care fence yesterday was still bugging me.

Maybe she was arranging day care for a child yet to be born, but I wasn't convinced. Her demeanor told me there was something else. It wasn't like she'd been interacting, talking to the child care workers and getting a feel for the place. She'd been hiding in the shadows, observing. I thought of Jonathan. He'd be about five years old now. The same age as many of the kids at the day care.

After a bottle of water and a shower I started on the path from my driveway to Rhea's. It was heady with the scent of lilacs, huge purple clusters dripping from overgrown bushes on either side. I stopped to break off a few of the largest blossoms so I wouldn't arrive empty handed. The flowers would be a preemptive peace offering for the way I planned to steer the conversation.

"Wow," Rhea said swinging back the kitchen door. "They're beautiful. Every once in a while, I catch the scent of them through the kitchen window. There's nothing better."

She took the bunch from my hand and walked to the sink. Extracting a large glass pitcher from an overhead cabinet, she filled it half full with water, slipped the stalks in and set it on the counter. "Picture perfect," she said. "Thanks. What brings you over? No work today?"

"Griff's doing some research so I opted for a workout and a late start."

"I miss working out." She lay her palm against her bulging stomach.

"Not much longer now."

"No, not much longer." Looking a little wistful, she slipped onto the stool beside me.

We sat at the kitchen counter in silence.

"Can I get you something?" she asked as though suddenly remembering I was there.

"No, I'm fine. How's your ankle?"

"Much better, thanks."

"That's what Griff said."

"What?"

"We saw you yesterday at the day care. We were driving by and you were watching the kids. Griff said your ankle must be better. That's kind of a long way to venture alone, isn't it? I mean being pregnant and having a bad ankle. You've got to be careful these days. You're so close."

"I'm not an invalid. I'm pregnant. I was out doing errands. I'll go mad if I just sit home and wait."

"You stopped to look at the kids?"

"I do that sometimes. I like to watch them play."

"Anticipation?" I asked nodding to her baby bulge.

She was quiet for a few moments, folded and unfolded her hands. Then she looked up at me. I knew what she was about to tell me, but I kept my mouth shut. I wanted to hear it from her.

"I lost a child," she said. "Jonathan would be five years old now."

"I'm so sorry."

"It was four years ago. You must have heard about it when it happened. It was all over the news. He was kidnapped."

"I don't know. I probably heard about it at the time, but I guess I've forgotten.

Can I ask what happened?"

"He was playing. Driving his toy cars around the living room floor. He'd just started walking, but crawling was still a faster mode of travel. He crawled around the rug with one hand on the floor for balance and the other propelling a car while he made little humming noises like an engine. Funny how little boys are all about sound effects," she smiled, but her eyes were far away, no doubt resting on that one-year-old boy crawling about on the living room rug.

"I'd stepped into the kitchen to make us lunch. It took no more than ten minutes. A dish of strawberry yogurt with mashed bananas and cut up grapes on the side. I always cut the grapes in half even though he had some teeth. Grapes are so easy to choke on."

I nodded.

"I'd been listening to him hum, you know, the car engine, so I knew he was fine, still playing. There were sweaters out on the back deck drying, but it had started to rain a bit so I stepped out the door to bring them in. It took no more than three or four minutes and I was back in the kitchen. I went to the counter and cut a few more grapes. It was then that I noticed the quiet. The humming had stopped. I set down my paring knife and went to the living room to check on him. He wasn't there. I figured he'd crawled down the hallway. I went everywhere throughout the house walking and calling, then running and screaming. He was nowhere. I even went upstairs though he'd never attempted to climb the stairs, but you know a one-year-old. They'll try anything if they want it badly enough."

Tears brimmed her eyes.

I reached out and laid my hands over hers to quiet her clenching and unclenching fists.

"And they never found him?" I asked.

She shook her head. "Mike's well known and well liked. The force did everything possible, called in the FBI. No one left a stone unturned, but Jonathan was never found."

"You must still hope?"

She nodded and smiled, her eyes full. "I only want to know that he's well and that he's loved."

"You don't think anything bad happened? You believe he's alive?"

"I'm sure of it." She smiled and patted my hand before pulling hers away.

"And you'd stopped to watch the kids yesterday because…"

"Because they make me think of him," she interrupted. "And watching the games they play lets me know what he's doing now too."

A little sick, I thought, but who wouldn't be a little sick after losing a child and never knowing if he was dead or alive?

"It must make you sad to watch them."

"It's bittersweet," she said. "In a way, it makes me feel closer to him. But each time I watch them my heart breaks a little more."

Okay, so I'm an unfeeling troll. I came over here hoping to uncover some long- buried twist regarding Jonathan's disappearance. The sight of her watching those kids had unleashed the skeptic in me. But by jumping to the conclusion there was more to it, I'd gnawed at a wound that will never fully close. My impulsiveness made a fool of me, a heartless one at that.

"I'm sorry, Rhea. I shouldn't have mentioned it."

"Not a day goes by that I don't think about him so you don't have to apologize. He's always just beneath my surface, his name on the tip of my tongue."

I glanced at the kitchen clock. It was almost eleven. "I'd better get to the office or Griff will have me putting in overtime."

"Of course." She smiled, but her eyes were weary. "How is it, working together?"

"It's great. We have a rapport." I slipped off the stool.

"I can't imagine it. I relish the moment Mike leaves for work and I have the house to myself."

"Maybe marriage changes things."

"It changes a lot," she said crushing a napkin in the palm of her hand.

Griff was staring at his lap top when I stepped into his office. Opened books and scattered papers lay strewn over his desk. "Find anything?" I asked.

"I'm taking a crash course in doping. There's a cornucopia of options. Including our prime suspects, EPO and amphetamines. Get this, if an athlete gets a transfusion prior to a race, it increases the number of red blood cells in their system. And, since red blood cells carry oxygen it increases the amount of oxygen in the body thereby increasing the runner's stamina and wind."

"That's what Gina said. You think Ashley was shooting up someone's blood?"

"It was the thing to do before EPO came into fashion. But the better way to go would have been a transfusion of her own blood. It would virtually go undetected. Nothing would look any different on autopsy or for that matter on any drug test."

"She draws her own blood then injects it back into herself?"

"She, or whoever was helping her, would draw two pints of her blood. That's the usual amount from what I've read. Then it's frozen. This could be done a couple of months prior to a race. In the meantime, her body would naturally replenish the blood loss. Just before the race the blood is injected back into her system thereby giving her an extra two pints of blood, boosting her red blood cell count and her oxygen level."

"And her hematocrit."

Griff nodded.

"That sounds a little over the top for a college athlete, a professional maybe.

"Just a thought. Blood-Doping was banned by the International Olympic Commission in 1985 and outlawed altogether in '86, but according to this," he pointed to a document on his desk. "It's coming under fire again. Although EPO seems to have pretty much taken the place of transfusions."

I slid the papers he was reading from his hand and sat down across from him, scanning the article. "Pretty interesting, but Gina didn't find any needle marks."

"Even on an intact body they can be hard to find. On Ashley, it would have been impossible."

"That's gross."

"That's fact. But drugs or needles weren't on anyone's mind when the autopsy was done, anyway. And if she was doping, I think she'd have chosen an area less likely to be noticed."

"Like between her toes? That's how they do it on *Law and Order*."

"I'm not up to par on injection sites, but I'm sure there are some options we'd never think of."

I tossed the papers back on his desk. "I went over to see Rhea this morning, to see how her ankle was."

He cocked his head to one side. "You're talking to me. And I know digging when I see it."

"Okay, I may have steered the conversation toward her lost child just a bit."

"Right. I know what your "bit" means," he said. "What did she say?"

"She told me about the day Jonathan disappeared. It sounded unbearable. She said she thinks about him every day."

"Hence why she was watching the kids at the playground."

I nodded.

He shook his head. "What'd I tell you?"

"Okay, okay. I won't do it again. I just thought…"

"Sometimes things are exactly what they look like. A dog is a dog."

"And sometimes what looks like a dog is really a wolf."

Eighteen

After wrestling with Rhea's story of Jonathan's disappearance and Griff's explanation of why she'd been standing in the shadows at the day care, I'd snagged a mere three hours of sleep. I begged off an early rising for a couple more hours of shuteye and Griff accommodated, begrudgingly. I don't think he cared that I wasn't coming with him to the office. I think he cared about the subject matter that was keeping me awake.

I heard the front door close and threw back the covers. Okay, so I lied. I wasn't staying home to sleep. I was staying home to think. In the kitchen, he'd left me a fresh pot of coffee. (There's no fooling Griff.) I poured a cup and slid onto a high back stool, resting my elbows on the counter top.

If the birth of my child was rapidly approaching (big if), I'd have a nursery ready, I'd be preparing make-ahead dinners for the freezer, I'd be in a dual state of high anxiety and intermingling excitement. Rhea was none of these things. In fact, the child didn't even have a room of its own. It would be sequestered in the guest room. The implications of which, were almost too frightening to consider. And she was spending time in the shadows, staring into a playground of four and five-year-olds.

Unless…I took a sip of coffee and dropped two slices of wheat bread into the toaster. Unless…I looked at the clock. Eight forty-five. The idea forming in my head was taking priority over my gurgling stomach. Irritated that I had to wait for toast when I had better things to do, I ran upstairs to the bathroom, swung the shower nozzle to hot and stepped in.

Back in the kitchen, ready to go, the toast was hard and dry. Nothing a slather of butter won't fix. With a napkin full of crumbs and a half full mug of lukewarm coffee I slipped into my SUV and turned the key.

At the intersection of Route 7 and Turner Avenue, The Blue Kangaroo Day Care came into view. I eased onto the shoulder of the road and turned off the engine. A couple of women were just coming out of the building after having left their kids. They chatted for a minute and then each went to her car. I crunched on my toast, washed it down with cold coffee and spotted a Daisy Donut up the road. After replenishing my caffeine fix, I returned to my vantage point across the street from the day care.

At eleven o'clock the door opened and a stream of little ones stampeded onto the playground. VI watched them for a while, one in particular, a little boy with unruly auburn hair, and with the help of my binoculars, a big smile. I wasn't ready to congratulate myself yet. Not until I noticed Rhea coming down the sidewalk on the opposite side of the street. "Shit," I whispered to no one, not sure that I wanted my hunch to pay off. She slipped under the same Maple tree and watched the children play. A half an hour later, the kids went back inside and Rhea left, walking slowly back to her car a few hundred feet away, under the weight of her sagging belly.

I stayed a bit longer trying to figure out what to do next. At 12:00 a school bus stopped out front and ten kids marched out of the day care and onto the bus. Kindergarten? What did I know, but it was a good guess. When the bus pulled away, I crossed the street and went inside.

"Can I help you?" A grandmother type looked up from a desk. Behind her the wall was decorated with an array of crayoned drawings.

"Hi, I'm new to the area. Just moved here, actually. I'm looking for a day care and my neighbor suggested I talk to you."

"Oh lovely, we're glad you stopped in."

She pulled a brochure from her drawer and began pointing out package options along with varying costs.

"Could I have a look around first?" I asked.

"Certainly," she said shoving the colored brochure back inside her desk understanding her mistake of putting money before the tour.

There were two large rooms. On the right, five toddlers were lying quietly on cushioned mats, some sleeping, some sucking their thumbs, wide-eyed.

"It's naptime," she explained. The older kids just left for kindergarten. They'll be back at three-o'clock."

To the left was the classroom with different stations spread around the room. There was a water table and a clay table, a Lego station, painting easels with smocks hanging off the wooden sides.

"Wow," I said to the slender woman behind the desk. "Pretty much anything a kid could want."

She laughed and brushed crumbs from her hands. I'd interrupted her lunch.

"Sorry, didn't mean to catch you at a bad time."

"No problem," she said coming toward me and shaking my hand. "I'm Devon Seyer."

"You're in charge of all this?"

"I have help. And you are?"

"Claire," I said. "Eastwood." (I have a thing for Clint Eastwood. It's the closest I'll ever get.) "I have a five-year-old and I need a day care that can get her to kindergarten."

"You've come to the right place. Have a seat."

After going over a typical day in the life of a day-care kindergartener, we discussed the number of kids in class, how they get along, the bus ride etc. All things I pretended I knew something about. Then I got to the real reason for my visit.

"My daughter was adopted," I said. "And she's very vocal about it. We've never shielded her from it in fact we encourage her to have a relationship with her birth mother. Sometimes, her birth mother accompanies us to special occasions, like school functions or in this case day care functions. I assume you have holiday parties?"

Devon nodded.

"Do you think that will be a problem for any of the other children? I mean, we've been to numerous groups for adoptive parents and I know some people have a problem when a child talks about adoption. They don't want their kids to be frightened by it."

"I don't think it will be a problem," Devon said. "Maybe you can explain to…what's your daughter's name?"

"Blake."

"…to Blake, that she not talk about it when she's here. But I don't see it as an issue. In fact, well…without divulging any details, we do have another child in the group that is adopted. But he doesn't talk about it."

Bingo.

There was a loud noise out in the hallway and I could hear someone calming a crying child.

"Excuse me," Devon said and walked out into the hall.

I glanced at her desk. There were a number of files and drawings, an appointment calendar and paper that said Weekly Roster. Beneath the heading was each day of the weak with a list of ten to fifteen names under each day. I could hear Devon talking softly in the hall. I slipped the paper off her desk and into my pocket in one sweep. My heart skipped a beat.

"I think I'm all set," I said coming into the hall behind Devon. "May I take a brochure from the front desk?"

"Of course," Devon said and nodded to the woman who I'd met initially.

"I hope we'll hear from you and Blake," she called after me.

I followed the other woman to the desk, took the brochure and got out of the day care as fast as I could without making my hurry obvious. I wondered how long it would take Devon to notice the missing roster and if she'd suspect anything or figure she misplaced it. I put my money on the latter.

I had just opened my car door when Rhea stepped up beside me.

"Checking up on me?"

"I, ah, I…no."

"You're a PI."

I nodded.

"You were checking up on me."

I nodded again.

"Why? What's going on in your head that would cause you to do this?"

"Get in. Let's talk."

Rhea looked at me, her lower lip clenched between her teeth. Sighing, she shook her head and walked slowly around the front of the RAV keeping her palm on the black metal for stability and making me wish I'd washed the car. She opened the passenger door, hefted her body onto the seat and sighed again.

I wracked my brain for some kind way of saying that I was following up on her story of Jonathan's disappearance without actually saying that I was following up on her story of Jonathan's disappearance.

"You don't believe what I told you about the day Jonathan disappeared?"

"I believe what you told me. I'm looking for answers."

"What makes you think you can find what the police and FBI were unable to?"

I shrugged. "Lunacy?"

She smiled and her body relaxed a little. "What did you go inside for?"

I slipped the roster from my bag and showed it to her.

"Jesus, Britt. That's confidential."

"I know."

"Do you really think one of those kids is Jonathan?"

"I don't know."

"Well, I do. He isn't there."

"But that one with…"

"The auburn hair like mine?" Rhea finished my question. "I wonder if that's what he looks like now. But it's not him. He's not there."

"How can you be sure?"

"Because I am." She turned her head and looked out the window.

I touched her arm. "Rhea, I know this is a horrible thing to say, but do you ever think that he might…"

"Be dead?" She asked, turning to look at me. "No."

"How can you be sure?"

"I just know. You don't need to look for him, Britt."

She opened the door, but hesitated. "Look, I appreciate the fact that you care, that you care enough to break some rules."

She nodded to the roster on the seat. "But I don't need your help."

"But, don't you…"

"No, Britt. I don't." She closed the door and walked away.

I beat Griff home and started the grill. In the kitchen, I marinated two chicken breasts and tossed salad fixings in a large wooden bowl. I'd just poured a glass of Pinot when he came through the back door.

"Where've you been all day? Katie said you were in and out of the office before I got back from my meeting."

"How'd the meeting go?" I asked changing the subject and buying time. I still hadn't decided if I was going to tell him what I'd done today. It had gnawed at me all afternoon that Rhea hadn't been thrilled by my interest in searching for Jonathan.

"…so I told him I'd discuss it with you and get back to him."

"Discuss what?"

"Taking the case."

"What case?"

"The one I just told you about."

"Sorry, my head was somewhere else. Can you tell me again?"

"The guy thinks his business partner's using the company as a cover to import stolen art."

"What kind of business is it?"

"International antique trade."

"Sounds interesting."

"Yeah, I told him I'd get back to him in a day or two. We've gotta wrap up the Lambert case."

"It feels like we're close with what Gina told us."

Griff nodded and went to the refrigerator for a beer. "You didn't answer me. Where were you all day?"

I've never kept anything from Griff and I didn't want to start now, especially not now. We'd begun a new chapter as they say, having bought a home together. It was the start of something. I wanted it to be the beginning of a future not the beginning of the end.

"I went back to the day care today."

He slid onto a bar stool at the counter and nodded, waiting for more, watching me dress the salad.

"Rhea was under the tree again."

He raised his eyebrows. A good sign, I thought. He's showing interest.

"She stayed and watched the kids for a while, like she did the other day." I set down the bottle and pushed the bowl aside. "There's a kid who looks just like her."

"What are you saying? He's her long-lost son?"

"I thought he might be. After she left I went inside and talked to the teacher."

"And?"

"I said I was new to the area and needed day care for my daughter. When she left the room I took the roster listing the children."

"You what?"

"That teacher's gonna get canned."

"She'll think she misplaced it and print another one. It's not a big deal."

"Jesus, Britt," Griff shook his head.

"The kid's the spitting image of Rhea." Griff didn't say anything so I kept talking, fast as though warding off a blow. "Why else would she be hanging around the day care?"

"What're you planning to do with this information?"

"Nothing right now. Rhea caught me."

He set his beer on the counter. "Nice. What'd she say?"

That she knows the kid looks like Jonathan, but it isn't him and that I don't need to look for him because she knows he's okay."

"She knows he's okay?"

"Yeah, isn't it kind of odd that she wouldn't take me up on an offer to reopen the search? Unless she knows he's all right because the kid at the day care is him. What do you think?"

"I think you've put your nose, yet again, where it doesn't belong. If Rhea knows something about her son's whereabouts then it's up to her to act on it or not. And the possibility of that little boy at the day care being Jonathan is so slim it's almost negligible. They looked for him for over a year and you think you just happened to stumble upon him a few miles from home?"

"Those things happen."

"On television."

"C'mon, Griff, why are you so against the possibility?"

"We're working a case that we need to finish up. We've now got another one on the threshold and we've just moved into a new house and are trying to make nice with the neighbors. Instead of focusing on these things, you're off on a wild goose chase to find a kid who's been missing for four years. Have you even thought of the pain and suffering you'll inflict? The wounds you'll reopen? Rhea and Mike have been through a major trauma. You want to make them re-live it because you have a hunch? Rhea told you to stop. Respect her wishes."

I felt like a trap door had opened beneath me. Deflated, I picked up my pinot and took a long swallow, digesting his words.

The doorbell rang and Griff went to get it. I followed along behind. Mike McKenzie was standing on the steps, his bike leaning against the porch railing.

"Hey you two, Rhea sent me over to invite you for dinner tomorrow night. You free?"

Griff glanced at me.

"We'd love to," I said. "What can we bring?"

"Just yourselves. Six o'clock. She has it all planned out. She's gotta have something to do hanging around the house all day."

He laughed.

I didn't.

"Great," Griff said. "We'll see you then."

We stepped back inside and Griff closed the door. He grabbed my hand and smirked. "Maybe you can tell Mike what you just told me over dinner."

I pulled away without answering, walked into the kitchen and topped off my Pinot. Then I went out to the deck, leaving the marinating chicken and the salad sitting on the kitchen counter. If he was hungry, let him cook.

Nineteen

I woke up hungry. Last night's uncooked chicken was sitting on the top shelf of the refrigerator when I reached in to get the half and half for my morning coffee. I hadn't heard or felt Griff get into bed last night even though I'd stayed up late reading, half hoping he'd come upstairs and half hoping he wouldn't. He'd already left for the office and I was feeling like shit.

We rarely fought. In fact, this may have been our first major disagreement. We'd had differences of opinion, but this felt bigger than that. The way I saw it, I was concerned with a woman's wellbeing, questions of abuse and the disappearance of her child, legitimate concerns for any friend and neighbor.

"Don't mix personal with professional," Griff always said.

But hadn't we mixed it six months ago when I went undercover to look for John Stark's daughter? I mean isn't Detective Stark Griff's best friend? Wasn't that a mix of personal and professional? I would remind him of that when I got to the office. That is, if we were speaking.

"Hey," Griff said.

He was standing by the fax machine when I opened the office door.

"Hey. Where's Katie?" I asked using her as a buffer.

"Went to Staples."

I nodded and walked into my office. I could feel him behind me. I opened the window, took a Honey Berry out of my pocketbook, lit it and sat on the fire escape, my legs dangling over the windowsill inside the office.

"You trying to piss me off?" Griff asked.

"No, just wanted a smoke."

"Sorry about dinner," he said.

"Me too."

"I didn't feel like cooking."

"Me either."

"We on for McKenzie's tonight?"

"Yeah."

"Britt." He looked at the floor, choosing his words. "I know you're concerned about Rhea and I will admit there are some things that seem a little off, but you don't know them well enough yet to be making such grand assumptions. The things you're suggesting are huge. Life changing. I'm not saying you're wrong to have questions and I agree it's strange that Rhea is so sure Jonathan's okay. But I am suggesting that you slow down. Let's enjoy dinner tonight and see how you feel after that."

I took a long drag on my cigar and blew the smoke in his general direction. (Okay, a little passive aggressive, nobody's perfect.) "Deal," I said.

He nodded and stepped out, closing my office door behind him.

I stubbed out what was left of my Honey Berry and scooted back inside.

I did a little more research on performance enhancers and how to beat drug testing. Then I read up on Jones and Lockridge, the company owned by the guy Griff had talked to about his not so honest business partner. At four o'clock, I called it day, an unproductive day, but a day none-the-less.

Griff was in the shower when I got home so I hit the elliptical making sure I would be stress free when I got to McKenzie's. No preconceived notions would come to dinner with me tonight. I was tabula rasa. We could put the pieces together when we got home. I had no doubt there'd be fuel for my fire. I just hoped the flames would be big enough for Griff to see.

At six o'clock we came through the path that led from our house to McKenzie's. Mike was out by the pool, the grill hot and smoking.

"Right on time," Mike said. "Beer and wine. Help yourself." He nodded to the table set for four.

An ice basket held a bottle of Pinot Grigio and the cooler on the floor was packed with a variety of microbrews. Griff popped the cork on the wine and poured me a glass then pulled an IPA from the cooler. Rhea appeared from the kitchen holding a

Scar Tissue

platter of fruit and cheese, a box of crackers tucked under each arm.

Mike swallowed half his beer and watched her come down the steps. I set down my wine and went to help her.

"Last thing we need is for you to take a spill," I said lifting the plate out of her hands.

"Thanks," she said. "It's almost time anyway."

"Yeah, but you don't want to go like that."

She laughed. "At this point I'm ready to go however it happens. The last month is a killer. I left my tea in the kitchen. Be right back."

"Let me get it," I said. "You sit down."

"It's on the counter by the sink."

I walked up the steps to get Rhea's tea already relegating Mike to asshole status. What kind of husband watches while his wife, in her ninth month of pregnancy, carrying shit in and out of the house, up and down the stairs? On the way back outside, I reminded myself to slow down, don't rush to judgment. That was the deal.

Mike threw four NY strip steaks on the grill and we took seats around the table, munching on cheese and crackers.

"You guys working on a case now?" Mike asked.

"Yeah," Griff said. "A young girl committed suicide, parents want to know why."

Mike set his beer on the glass top table, his eyes on Griff. "You're not talking about Ashley Lambert, are you?"

"You knew her?"

Mike drew his mouth in a fine line. "I know her mother. She's my step-sister."

I looked at Mike then at Griff. Gwen's lowlife stepbrother named Michael. What the hell?

"You're Gwen's step-brother?" Griff asked obviously as surprised as I was.

Mike nodded. "The step-brother from hell, according to her. Her family didn't acknowledge me, to say the least. I was an embarrassment. I guess it's understandable since her father, our father, was unfaithful. They were one of those families who believed if you didn't talk about it, it didn't happen. Needless to say, my name was rarely mentioned."

"Wow," I said. "This is crazy. Did you know Ashley?"

"No. I never met her. Read about her occasionally in the newspaper. I understand she was quite the athlete."

"She was," Griff said. "And an exceptional student, which is why her death is so difficult to understand."

"No note?" Mike asked.

"Nothing," Griff said.

"You sure it was suicide?" Mike asked, the cop in him creeping out. He got up to flip the steaks and put a baked potato on each plate then took the plastic wrap off the salad in the middle of the table. (Redeeming himself ever so slightly).

"Autopsy says so."

"They did an autopsy after a fall like that? Couldn't have been much to work with."

"Her father wanted it."

"Good old Greg," Mike said.

"You know him?" I asked.

"Not really. I remember him a little from when we were kids. Met him once or twice when I was actually in their house. But that was rare. Like I said, I wasn't their favorite person. Greg was a dick then. What's he like now?"

"Same," I said.

Mike laughed.

"They do a tox screen?"

"Just the standard," Griff said.

"Show anything?"

"No results yet," Griff said fast, like he'd wanted to get that out before I could say anything.

I glanced at him. He met my eyes with a look that told me he was choosing how much to say. I let him take the lead.

"We're looking into the possibility of drugs. Like you said, she had everything going for her. Suicide doesn't make sense, although it is ruled as cause of death. We're wondering if drugs could have affected her thinking."

Mike nodded as he put a sizzling steak on each of our plates and sat down. "Worth looking into," he said. Then he raised his beer, "To kids and the parents who fuck 'em up." He glanced at Rhea.

Her eyes were on her glass of iced tea, sweating on the table.

"Maybe you can give us a little insight," Griff said.

"In what sense?" Mike asked, spearing a piece of steak with his fork.

"Performance Enhancers, you were a pro-cyclist weren't you?"

"Yeah, but I never touched the stuff. Hence, I'm not a pro anymore. Sank to the amateur level, but I'm clean."

"Did you know anybody that used them?"

"Lots of guys."

"Mind if I ask you about it?"

"Shoot."

I gave Griff the alpha position in this conversation. I figured Mike might be more into it if it were man to man. He seemed like that kind of guy. Like I wouldn't be smart enough to understand what he had to say, but another guy was on his level.

"I was reading about blood doping."

"Yeah, that's kind of old school now. I mean there are still guys that do it because it's easy if you're using your own stash. It used to go undetected, but the testing is savvier now and a high hematocrit raises a red flag. You think she was doping?"

"I'm not sure. What do you know about EPO?"

"Erythropoietin," Mike said. "Does the same thing as doping, but with a lot less mess." He smiled. "It's popular, but again it raises flags due to the hematocrit level on tests. It's getting tougher to be a user, that's for sure. WADA's cracking down."

"WADA?" I asked.

"World Anti-Doping Agency."

"How hard is it to get this stuff?"

"For a college kid? I'd say it would be difficult. If you're in the pro-circuit that's one thing, but for a college athlete, I'm not sure she'd have the connections. I mean, maybe she did. I don't know who she hung around with, but my guess is that college athletes are more into amphetamines. They've gotta be easy to find on campus."

Griff nodded. "Yeah, that's been our thinking too. That is if anything shows up on toxicology."

"Let me know when you get it back. I mean, if I can be of any help."

"Will do," Griff said, refilling my Pinot and grabbing another beer for himself and a fourth one for Mike.

"Can I get you something?" I asked Rhea. "More tea?"

"No thanks, I'm fine," she said.

She hadn't said two words since we'd arrived and I wondered if something had happened between her and Mike. They'd hardly looked at each other all evening. I stood to clear our empty plates.

"I've got that," Rhea said.

"No really, let me carry them in."

"Well, I'll come with you and get desert."

I followed her up the stone stairway and into the kitchen. "You okay? You seem quiet."

She shrugged. "Yeah, I'm fine."

"You're always quiet when Mike's around." The words came out of my mouth before I thought to filter.

"You've noticed."

"Hard not to."

"He doesn't always give much credence to what I have to say, especially in front of guests. He likes to be the one in the know. I've learned to say very little when we have company, it protects me from being embarrassed."

"That's awful."

"That's life with my husband." She picked up an apple pie from the counter and slipped it into a pre-heated oven. "Warm in here," she said and slipped off the sweater she'd been wearing outside.

The gasp was out of my mouth before the sleeves were fully off her arms, no reining it in. "Rhea, what happened?" But I knew before she answered. A thick black smudge on each bicep, with four navy blue extensions encircling her skin, like a slave bracelet or a perfectly tattooed handprint. "He held you down."

"Shit," she said and slipped her sweater back on. Then she looked at me, her eyes holding my own even as they brimmed with tears. "Britt…"

I held up my hand. "I know. I knew the first day we met. There's something unmistakable about an abused woman. I've seen it too many times."

"Hey, what's a guy have to do to get a little pie around here?" Mikes voice came up the steps from the deck.

"You've got to get help, Rhea."

"From who? He's one of the most well-liked cops on the force. You think his buddies will come down on him? Nobody breaks the code. And I have no one else. No family, no money, a high school education."

"Well you've got me now. We'll figure it out. How long has this been going on?"

"Things used to be good between us. His temper has always been an issue, but he wasn't physical. That came later. He started pushing me around a little, getting right in my face when we'd argue." She sighed and shook her head. "Then one day he backhanded me. It's only gotten worse since then."

"What's going on in there?" It was Mike again.

"I'm coming," Rhea called and slid the pie from the oven. "Grab the ice cream in the freezer," she nodded to me. "Hurry, I have to get out there. He'll think we're talking."

"What the hell's wrong with talking?"

"He doesn't like it." She hurried toward the door.

"Things are gonna change around here," I said more to myself than to her.

As Rhea went through the door she glanced back at me. She'd heard what I said and I couldn't tell if it was hope or fear on her face, but my money was on the latter.

"What the hell you two doing in there?" Mike asked.

There was an irritated undertone in his voice. I hoped Rhea wouldn't pay later.

"This looks great," I said, scooping ice cream onto plates beside the pie, hoping to shift Mike's focus onto the homemade dessert.

"Haven't had apple pie in ages," Griff said. "This is a treat."

"She's got nothin' else to do." Mike cracked another beer.

"She will soon," I said.

"Yeah, not much longer now." Mike looked at his wife.

It was a strange look. No hint of a smile or wink of acknowledgement of the birth they'd soon share. Just a steady gaze, unnerving and making me wish we didn't have to leave her alone with him.

Griff took his last bite, leaned back and patted his stomach. "That was delicious, Rhea. Maybe you can give Britt your recipe. No wonder you're a cyclist," he said to Mike. "You have to be to stay in shape with dinners like this all the time."

"See," I said. "I'm doing you a favor. Think of all the exercise time I'm saving you since I can't cook."

That got a smile from Rhea.

I helped her carry the dessert plates into the kitchen, but this time we didn't speak though I did squeeze her hand on the way back outside trying to convey the fact that she wasn't alone anymore. Mike was opening another beer when we got back to the table.

"Another one?" Rhea said.

"What're you my mother?" he asked.

She slipped into her chair.

Mike set a bottle in front of Griff.

Griff raised his hand. "I'm good, thanks. Everything was wonderful, but Britt and I have an early morning." He pushed his chair back from the table and I followed suit.

"Thanks, Rhea," I said. "I'll give you a call. Maybe we can do lunch at my house on Saturday. I make a mean grilled cheese."

"I'll vouch for that," Griff said. "Her specialty."

With a wave, we went through the gate and entered the path. I've never been so glad, or so hesitant to leave a dinner party.

Twenty

Griff closed our kitchen door behind him and leaned against it, looking at me. "Okay," he said. "I've been swayed to your way of thinking."

"What do you mean?"

"Well, I went there tonight hoping that by the time we left you'd be convinced that you were overreacting about Mike. Instead, I see why you're concerned about Rhea. The way he talks to her, the way he looks at her and I don't think she said more than five words all evening."

"She's got black and blue handprints on her arms."

"What?"

"I saw them when we went in to get dessert. She didn't mean for me to, but she took off her sweater and realized it too late."

"You ask her?"

"I didn't need to. I told her she needed to get help, but with him on the force it's close to impossible. At least that's how she sees it."

"But you can help her, connect her to someone?"

I nodded. "Of course. When I mentioned lunch, that's what I had in mind."

"You think she's ready to do something about it?"

"She has to. She can't subject a child to that kind of household because..."

The comment stopped me mid-sentence. I looked at Griff. "Do you think...?"

"Mike had something to do with Jonathan's disappearance?" Griff said completing my thought.

"Yeah, do you think the cops could have covered it up? I mean if he hurt Jonathan?"

"It's a possibility, I guess, but the Portland PD weren't the only ones involved. The FBI was in on it too. They'd have no sense of loyalty to Mike."

"Still..."

"It's something to keep in mind, I suppose. But then why was Rhea so sure that Jonathan is okay?" Griff went to the sink and poured himself a tall glass of water. "Not to change the subject, but what are the chances that Mike is Gwen's stepbrother?"

"Yeah, that was a little crazy, huh? Small world."

"He sure bore the brunt of his father's indiscretions. I mean it wasn't Mike's fault that his father was sleeping around."

"They had to blame someone. You sticking up for him?"

"No, no, I'm just pointing out that maybe Mike has an axe to grind."

"Against Gwen?"

Griff nodded. "What if Mike knew about Ashley's use of amphetamines or EPO?"

"He said he never met her."

"He lied. What if he was blackmailing Gwen? What if he was going to spill the beans on Ashley if Gwen didn't pay him? It would have ruined Ashley's future if that came out. She'd have lost her athletic status and her acceptance to Johns Hopkins. Greg would have walked and Gwen's happy family façade would have crumbled."

"Not a bad theory. How do we prove it?"

"Let's pay Gwen a visit in the morning. But right now, I have other things on my mind."

"Like what?"

"Like making it up to you that I didn't support your hunch about Mike in the first place."

"What have you got in mind?"

"If you come upstairs with me, I'll show you."

"Always have to keep me guessing, don't you?"

"Keeps me interesting."

"No, it's what you're going to show me upstairs that keeps you interesting."

In the morning, after coffee and Griff's blueberry pancakes, we headed for the Lambert's one more time. I wasn't looking forward to interrogating Gwen about being blackmailed by her stepbrother, but it was a definite possibility.

"You think she'll admit to it?" I asked.

"If Greg's not home, our chances will be better. It'll explain the $8,000 cash withdrawal out of Ashley's account every month."

"Did Gwen have access to that account?"

"I didn't think so, but that's something we should clarify."

"If Gwen was paying off Mike and Ashley knew about it, it would explain why she jumped too. Her death would have put an end to Mike's ability to blackmail Gwen."

"I hope we're wrong," Griff said killing the engine in front of Lambert's.

When no one answered the doorbell, we walked around the back of the house. Gwen was kneeling beside one of the raised flowerbeds.

"Gwen," I called, not wanting to startle her as we approached. She looked up and then slowly stood.

"Sorry, no one answered the door so we thought we'd check out here for you."

"Do you have news?"

"Maybe," I said. "Is Greg here?"

"He's at the club."

Good, I thought, but didn't say it.

"Have a seat." She motioned us to the wicker furniture.

"We spoke to Greg a few days ago about Ashley's financial situation," Griff said. "He told us she had a checking account and we've followed up with the bank. Did you have access to that account also?"

"No. I put money in occasionally, but Greg handled deposits most of the time. Ashley handled the rest. The statements went to her, I believe. Why do you ask?"

"There was a large cash withdrawal being made on the first of each month. Do you know anything about that?"

"No. How much was it for?"

"Eight thousand dollars," Griff said.

"What? What could she possibly have needed that for?"

"That's what we're trying to find out."

"We met your stepbrother, Mike, last night," I said.

Gwen looked at me like I'd just risen from the dead. "How could that be?"

"He's our new neighbor. We had dinner with him and his wife. We had no idea who he was until he asked us about the case we were working on. He told us he's your stepbrother. Did you know he's a cop in Portland?"

Gwen nodded. "I see his name in the paper occasionally. I don't pay much attention to it."

"I assume Greg told you about the results of the tox screen?" Griff asked.

Gwen nodded.

"We started thinking that if Mike knew Ashley was using drugs, he might use it as a way to get back at you for the way he was treated as a kid, ignored, snubbed, belittled. He's got a pretty nice house for a cop's salary. He's getting a boost from somewhere."

"You think he's been blackmailing me?" Gwen let out a raspy laugh. "I wouldn't give that little bastard a dime. He destroyed our family."

I wanted to point out that her father had done that all by himself, but instead said, "From Mike's perspective, it wasn't his fault he was born, but everyone treated him like it was. It makes sense that he'd want some payback."

"It makes sense, but it didn't happen," Gwen said.

"Could he have been blackmailing Ashley?"

"If he was in contact with my daughter, she would have told me."

"The further we get into this, the more we find things she didn't tell you.

I think that's something you need to start accepting."

"I think we're done here," Gwen said standing. "You're right that Michael is capable of that sort of behavior, but you're wrong to think any of us would have gone along with it. Do I need to show you out or can you find your way back the way you came?"

"I think we can manage," Griff said. "But if you want us to get the answers you're paying us for we need you and Greg to be more open to the possibility that Ashley may have been into things you weren't aware of."

"When you deliver a possibility worth considering, I'll look at it. Until then, keep digging."

"Ouch," Griff said as we made our way around the mini-mansion and back to the driveway.

"Yeah, didn't exactly go the way I was hoping, but I still think we're onto something."

We drove back towards Portland over the Casco Bay Bridge.

"You coming into the office?" Griff asked.

"I thought I might go home and check in on Rhea. I got the feeling Mike wasn't too pleased with her last night."

"She didn't do anything wrong that I could see."

"We were talking too long in the kitchen. She said he doesn't like that."

"Jesus, control or what?"

"That's the name of the game."

Twenty-Two

Griff dropped me off at the front door and drove back down the driveway heading for the office. Behind me dust swirled, the Land Rover's tires kicking up dirt. We needed rain. My phone rang before I unlocked the front door. Leaving the keys hanging in the lock, I looked at my cell. I couldn't place the number on the screen, but I'd seen it before.

"Hello?"

"Britt? It's Rhea. Can you come over? And bring your car."

"What's wrong?"

No answer.

"Rhea, are you okay?"

"Just come. Hurry."

Instead of unlocking the door, I pulled the keys out of the lock and fished around the ring for my car key. Inside the Rav, I tossed my bag onto the passenger seat, revved the engine and sped down the driveway, setting the dust in motion once again.

I ran up to Rhea's back door taking the stone steps two at a time and pushed inside. Rhea wasn't in the kitchen.

"Rhea," I yelled. "Where are you?"

I hurried through the stainless-steel kitchen, stepping over the array of broken plates and breakfast food that littered the floor.

"Rhea," I called again.

In the living room, a mirror hanging on the far wall had been shattered. The culprit, a brass candlestick, lay on the floor beneath it.

"Rhea, answer me."

"I'm here," came a voice slightly above a whisper.

She was sitting on the top step of the stairs, leaning against the rod iron railing.

"I think I'm in labor," she said.

"Where's Mike?"

"At work."

"Have you called him?"
"Have you looked around?"
I didn't say anything.
"I'll call him from the hospital," she said.
"Okay, let's go."

I helped her into the car and took off, praying that I would not be delivering this child on the front seat. It was a twenty-minute ride to Maine Medical Center. I had time to ask her what happened but wasn't sure the timing was right.

"Are you okay? I mean, not as far as the baby goes, but you, yourself. Did he hurt you?"

She gritted her teeth and I thought for a minute that was my answer, but then her body seemed to relax and she looked out the window.

"Contraction?"

She nodded. "He punched me."

"In the stomach?"

"I think that's what started the contractions. I'm not sure if it's the real thing or a reaction to being hit."

"What the f...? What's wrong with him?"

She shook her head. "Where should I begin? The least little thing sets him off. I keep thinking if I can make the perfect home he'll have less to get mad about, but he always finds something. It's become worse since Jonathan... He blames me. He always will. You must think I'm a fool. But I..."

Ahead of us the sign for the hospital's emergency entrance came into view. I pulled into the lot and up to the electronic front doors.

"Rhea, you don't have to explain. I'm not judging you. From everything you've told me, you were a wonderful mother. You loved Jonathan. But we better finish this later. You need to get inside."

"Wait," she put her hand on mine. "Jonathan's disappearance wasn't my fault.

It was my doing. I orchestrated it." She winced as another contraction hit.

I stared at her not sure I'd heard right and wanting the contraction to hurry up and end, so I could clarify what she'd said. A pounding on the window startled me and I turned from

Rhea to see who'd caused the disruption. A nurse stood at my door.

"Do you need help?" he said.

I looked back at Rhea, still in the midst of the contraction and me in the midst of disbelief. "Yes, I need help," I said opening my door. "She's in labor."

The nurse went to Rhea's side of the car, opened the door and helped her out and into a wheelchair.

"Go park the car," he said to me and meet us inside."

I followed his orders, still more inside my head than in the moment. In the parking garage, I took my ticket, slipped into a space and followed the signs back to the emergency room. On the way, I called Griff.

"He what?"

"You heard right. In the stomach."

"Has she called the police?"

"No and she won't. But I don't want to get into that now. I can talk with her later. I just want to make sure she's okay. I'm probably not coming into work."

"I should have believed you from the start."

"Yes, you should have. See you tonight."

Rhea was lying on a bed inside a curtained alcove when I got back. A doctor was speaking to her while a new nurse hooked up an ultrasound machine beside the bed. After running the wand over her stomach and watching the monitor, the doctor declared Braxton Hicks contractions or false labor.

"Your baby's head is still upright," he said pointing to the screen.

I inched closer, mesmerized by the image on the monitor, a baby, perfectly formed, sucking its thumb, floating in its own little surreal world.

"No signs of distress," the doctor said. "What's this from? He asked brushing his fingers lightly over a purplish, yellow mottling on Rhea's stomach.

"I tripped on the stairs this morning. I was carrying some books," she said.

He met her eyes with a look that said to me he wasn't buying it. "When are you due?"

"A week," Rhea said.

"Are you safe at home?"

"I'm fine. Really, I tripped. I'm pretty clumsy these days." She tried to laugh, but her smile fell away too fast.

The doctor turned to me. "And you are?"

"Her neighbor."

"Maybe you can look in on her? Make sure she's okay?"

There was an understanding in the exchange. An unstated knowledge that we both knew the truth about Rhea's circumstance and an agreement that I would try to protect her.

"Of course."

"You can go home, but rest today. No chores. Put your feet up. Some herbal tea should help. Make sure you're getting plenty of fluids."

I left Rhea in a wheelchair on the sidewalk, an aide standing beside her, and ran to the garage to get the car. On my way to pick her up my stomach flip-flopped in anticipation of finishing our conversation about Jonathan. I wasn't sure if she'd regret what she'd said. Sometimes pain and fear make people more vulnerable. Now that she was feeling better, she may feel like she said too much.

I helped her into the car and we drove in silence for a while.

"Do you want to stop for anything?" I asked. "Something to eat? Do you have herbal tea at home?"

"I'm all set, Britt," she said. "Do you want to hear the rest of it? I feel like I need to explain, I want to really. It's just…"

She searched my face and I returned the gesture the best I could while driving.

"Just what?" I asked.

"You can never tell anyone, not even Griff. It would destroy my life and the lives of my children."

It didn't elude me that she'd just said children. "I promise, Rhea," I said. "You can tell me whatever you need to. It'll never go further than this car." I wasn't sure that was true. I couldn't imagine not sharing whatever she was about to say with Griff, but I could decide that later.

"I arranged Jonathan's disappearance. Mike's abuse had escalated after Jon was born. He was jealous of my time with him, angry that I catered to a baby instead of him. When I found fingerprints on Jonathan's arm, I knew I had to do something. I couldn't go to the police for obvious reasons. If I tried to disappear he'd have found me. He has all the connections. So I got the idea that I would give Jonathan away."

I pulled into Rhea's driveway and turned off the engine. Neither of us moved.

"I decided that I would give him to someone else to raise as their own. I found a couple who run an underground adoption agency. It's a fast track for wealthy, European parents who want a healthy baby. I know that sounds horrible, but at least I knew he'd have everything he needed. I won't tell you how I found them or who they are, but I went through channels I trust. They assured me he would go to a safe and loving home. I believed them. I still do. I know he has a good life. Mike will never be able to lay a hand on him. I did the right thing."

Her cheeks were wet and I leaned across the seats to hug her. "I can't imagine how it must have broken your heart to give him up."

"It did then and it does every day, but I did it for him. I loved him so much. I still think of him as mine."

"Mike never suspected?"

"No, he thinks I wasn't watching him and someone came in and took him. No one ever suspected that I was involved. Mike being on the force helped, they looked at us a little in the beginning, but not for long. I guess you could say I got away with it, but it hasn't left me, not even for a second."

"The first time we came and looked at the house," I said, "I thought I heard someone in the woods calling for Jonathan."

She smiled a weary smile. "Sometimes I walk in the woods and talk to him so Mike won't hear me. I sing him songs and tell him how much I love him."

She started to cry and I held her while she struggled with a sadness I could only imagine. Giving up a child she cherished to live with a man she hated. All in the name of love.

"C'mon," I said. "Let's go inside. You get in the bath and I'll clean up."

I considered all that Rhea had told me as I pushed a mop over the kitchen floor. I think I would have opted for running away after the first punch, but I also understand the fear that's involved with escaping an abuser and how many women are killed in the midst of leaving. It's easy to say what you'd do when you're not in the position. I'd just come back inside from delivering the trash bag with the mirror and glass to the barrel in the garage when Rhea came downstairs in her bathrobe.

"I can't thank you enough for all this," she said.

"No need to." And then I asked the question that had been nagging at me since she'd gone upstairs. "What about this one?" I placed my hand on her stomach and looked at her. "What will you do?"

"I'm leaving Mike this time. I've had nine months to plan it. I'm going to disappear with my baby. I've put away money. I'm not afraid anymore. I won't give up another child because of him. I just have to wait until I'm strong again."

"I'll help you when the time comes," I said.

She put her hand over mine. "I'm counting on it."

Twenty-Three

I was sautéing shrimp and vegetables on the stove for dinner when I first heard what sounded like someone turning the knob on the back door. Griff had called an hour earlier to tell me he was taking Allie out for pizza. I'd opted for a quick stir-fry for myself. I glanced at the back hallway. A stack of five or six boxes we'd yet to unpack stood against the door. No one was getting in that way.

I heard the noise again, lowered the heat under the wok and moved cat quiet toward the backdoor trying to dismiss the pounding of my heart. I flipped on the outside light fast and peered through the darkened glass, hoping to catch an intruder by surprise. There was no one there. I exhaled, reminding myself that out here, noises on your porch didn't necessarily mean a break in. More likely, a visit from the neighborhood raccoons.

I poured a glass of Pinot Grigio and spooned some of the stir-fry onto a plate. Sitting at the kitchen counter alone my eyes wandered to the back hallway and I wished I'd taken Griff up on his offer to join him and Allie. I was still getting my country feet under me, still getting comfortable with the dark and the quiet. Or not. I glanced toward the back door again.

"Okay, cut the shit," I coached myself. "There's nothing out there."

After the last bite of cashew shrimp, I put my plate in the sink and went to the refrigerator for another splash of liquid courage. Then I headed to the stairs for a shower and my yoga pants before settling in to wait for Griff. I still hadn't decided whether or not to fill him in about Jonathan. Griff was as trustworthy as they came, but a crime had been committed, an illegal adoption, and there was abuse happening right next door. He might feel it his obligation as a law-abiding PI to lay things on the table.

I stepped into the shower stall and put my head under the spray of hot water. There's nothing like a hot shower to relieve anxiety. I poured my new mango body wash onto a loofa and ran it over my skin washing off the day's grime. I'd installed a gauzy curtain that ran the length of the shower's glass wall. It didn't hurt the unique layout, but it blurred the view from the outside. Amy had said only a crazy person would be hanging around in the woods peering into our shower. In my line of work, I knew she was right. I leaned my head under the spray rinsing shampoo from my hair and tipped my face letting the suds slide off my cheeks. When I opened my eyes, I saw the light. One beam flickering between the trees and moving through the woods at the edge of our backyard.

I grabbed a towel from the hook at the end of the stall and slipped around the tiled partition. Staying well behind the wall, I leaned back around to look into the yard. The light flashed over the deck, up the side of the house and past the gauzy curtain into the shower stall. My heart dropped to my stomach. Whoever it was, was coming toward the house.

I slipped into my yoga pants and pulled a Red Sox sweatshirt over my head. My cell phone was in my bag in the kitchen. I needed to get to it before whoever was out there came inside. I ran down the stairs trying to remember if I'd locked the front door when I got home. In the kitchen, I dumped my bag onto the counter and reached for my phone just as the knob turned on the back door.

I watched as whoever was on the other side pushed the door with enough force so that the boxes stacked in front of it moved smoothly over the tiles as the door opened.

Mike clicked off his flashlight and stepped into the dim light of our back hallway. "Hey neighbor," he said and swayed, his shoulder bouncing off the wall beside him.

"Locks these days really suck." He laughed and held up the Swiss Army knife in his hand. "You can open 'em with next to nothing. I keep tellin' people, you gotta have a deadbolt if you want to keep the riff-raff out."

"What do you want Mike?" I tried to keep my voice steady and not betray the fear spiking through me. This guy beat the shit out of his wife. What would he do to me?

"I want you to stay the hell out of my life," he said taking a few steps into the kitchen.

I stood my ground wishing I had my Charter Arms Pink Lady with me, but I'd locked it in the safe at work. "Your wife needed help," I said.

"When my wife needs help, I'll take care of her."

"It looked like you already did."

"You little bitch, know-it-all." He took a step and swayed again, reached out for the counter and steadied himself.

"Mike, go home. You're drunk."

"What you don't know is that my wife is a loser." He said the last word with such force his body jerked against one of the stools causing it to rock on its wooden legs. "She loses things…like children. Anybody who loses their kid deserves this." He raised a fist.

"She didn't lose Jonathan. Someone took him."

"How the hell do you know his name?"

"I read the papers. I know what happened. Someone kidnapped him from your house."

"She was home."

"You look away for a second and someone can steal your kid. It happens all the time. You're a cop. You know that."

"It doesn't happen to my kid. Not in my house."

"Being a cop doesn't make you immune."

"It makes me anything I want it to."

"Like an abuser? You beat your wife and then hide behind your badge?"

"Fuck you."

"No Mike, fuck you. If Rhea needs help, I'm going to help her. You're not going to scare me away."

"No?"

He walked across the kitchen to where I was standing and put his hand around my neck pushing me backwards. I reached out to grab something and knocked a stool to the floor. He shoved me hard against the wall. I turned my head away from his booze breath.

"Stay the fuck outta my house. Or we can play that little shower scene again only this time in person. That curtain you put up doesn't do you justice."

I brought my knee up fast and hard not sure where my aim was going to land. But he'd touched a nerve. I caught him off center. Not the direct hit I'd hoped for, but it caused enough pain to make him let go of my neck and take a few unsteady steps back.

"Get the fuck out of my house," I said grabbing the flashlight from the floor where he'd dropped it.

Both his hands were on his crotch. I hammered the flashlight into his chest hard enough to leave a bruise and he stumbled backwards thrown off balance by the abundance of booze in his gut. If he hadn't been drinking I'd have never gotten the upper hand. He grabbed the counter, but before he could steady himself I drove the flashlight into his chest again. This time he landed against the back door.

He grabbed for the knob and got his feet under him then raised his wild eyes to me. "You fucking come near my house again, you'll wish for the rest of your life you hadn't."

He backed out the door and onto the porch, his eyes still holding mine. I threw the flashlight onto the porch with him.

"Ditto," I said and slammed the door.

My fingers trembled with the lock. Knees giving out, I sank to the floor. Long slow breaths I coached, remembering what the doctor had told Rhea. The shaking subsided and my heart settled back to a normal beat. An hour later Griff walked in. I hadn't touched anything. The stool was still on the floor. So was I.

"What the hell...Britt." He knelt down next to me and put his arms around me. "What happened?"

On the couch with another glass of wine, I went over the whole day with him. I left nothing out. I'd told Rhea that I wouldn't tell, but after Mike's visit tonight, Griff needed the full story. And I would have told him anyway. No secrets.

"I'm going to nail him," Griff said standing up. Nobody comes into this house threatening you."

"No Griff." I stood and took his arm. "You can't."

"I can and I am. That bastards going to pay."

"He'll take it out on Rhea. She'll be the one to bear the brunt of it, not him. If you call the police, it's her word against his. Who're they going to believe?"

"It's our word too."

"I kneed him in the groin and hit him twice with a flashlight. He'll charge me with assault."

"It was inside our house. You were protecting yourself."

"And he's a cop. The whole thing will be a fucking mess. It's not worth it. Not right now. Rhea has a plan to leave him. Anyway, we want to look at him for his involvement in Ashley's death. If we find a connection none of this will matter. He'll be put away for a long time and Rhea will be safe. We keep digging. He's involved somehow, regardless of what Gwen says."

"Rhea can at least get a restraining order. Maybe we should too."

"You think he won't break it if he wants to?"

Griff stuffed his fists into the pockets of his jeans as though trying to keep them contained. "She gave her kid away?" He looked at me incredulous.

"Because she loved him. She didn't want him to have the life she has."

"I can't understand why women don't leave these bastards."

"No one can, but being beaten does a number on your head. And the fear can be immobilizing."

"So, we let him beat the shit out of her right next door? I can't do that."

"She has a plan to leave him as soon as the baby is born. We help her get away and when she's safe in a place where he won't find her then we go after him. She's due any day. We'll get him when the time is right and he'll pay. Believe me, he's not walking away from this. But we need to play it right so Rhea gets out safely."

Twenty-Four

The next morning my neck was sore, and I winced with each swallow of coffee, but I didn't let on to Griff. Why beat a dead horse? Things had to stay status quo for now. The more routine everything seemed, the less suspicious Mike would be. But I sure as hell wasn't staying away from Rhea. If she called I'd be there.

"I'm heading over to talk to Coach Massett," Griff said tossing the crust from his toast into the sink.

"Crust is good for your teeth."

He picked it back out of the sink and held it up. "You want it?"

I curled my lip at him. "I ate mine."

"You want to come?" he asked tossing the crispy edge into the disposal.

"Are you upset with me?"

"Not with you, with everything else."

I wrapped my arms around his waist. "You're a good man."

"I hate not retaliating for the way he treated you. I also hate leaving Rhea over there alone. I don't feel like a good man on either count."

"Mike's at work now. She's safe for today."

"I don't want him to think he's getting away with what he did to you last night."

"I'm sure in the back of his mind he knows you won't let that slide. So maybe not doing anything right now is better. It'll make him squirm."

"Thanks for pointing out the silver lining, Pollyanna, but I'm not sure it helps."

I ignored his remark. Even Griff gets to have a bad day once in a while. "C'mon, let's go see the coach, that'll take your mind off Mike McKenzie."

On the way to Fensworth College we passed the Royal Oaks new development.

"Looks like they've almost finished the pool," I said. "Just have to pour the cement."

"Better hurry up or they'll have to wait until next summer to use it."

"That's when we'll be using ours." I smiled at him.

"Got that right. We'll break ground in the spring."

"Something to look forward to when the snow's up to my knees."

"A miserable winter makes us appreciate summer that much more."

"Is that a silver lining?"

Griff laughed. "Wise ass."

At Fensworth we pulled straight back to the athletic complex. It was early so the track and surrounding grounds were still empty. Inside the field house we wandered the corridor reading the embossed names on each door. Third door on the left was Coach Massett, Track and Field. We knocked.

"Yeah." Came from the other side.

Griff opened the door and the coach looked up from a desk piled high with magazines and spiral notebooks.

"Hey, Coach," Griff said. "We've got a few more questions. You mind?"

"Have a seat." He motioned to a green vinyl couch pushed against the wall. A pile of jerseys took up one of the cushions.

"Shove those on the floor," he said. "They're dirty anyway."

I sat on the edge of the couch and Griff took the arm.

"Toxicity screen came back," Griff said.

Massett raised his eyebrows.

"Ashley Lambert had amphetamines in her system and there's a question of EPO or blood doping because her hematocrit was higher than the normal range."

Coach Massett took off his glasses and tossed them onto his desk. "Not on my team."

"The tests don't lie."

"Labs have been wrong before."

"How often was she tested at competitions?"

"I told you, once in a while at a tournament, but testing is relatively rare in college sports."

"Why is that?" I asked.

Coach Massett stood and took a breath then walked to the small window in his office overlooking the soccer field. "People don't want to know at the college level. You get a pro that's better than everyone around him and nobody trusts him. Professionals are tested up the yin-yang. But a college kid who's doing great? Everyone just wants to cheer them on. It's psychological. We still think of college athletes as our kids. And we all want to support our children's success. Testing is sporadic at best." He turned and looked at Griff. "EPO? You sure?"

"The test was inconclusive, but the suspicion is there because of the high hematocrit. No question on the amphetamines though."

Coach Massett shook his head and stared at the pile of dirty jerseys still on the couch. "Jesus," he said. "This gonna come out to the public?" He looked up, the concern plain on his face.

"That's up to the family," Griff said. "But I doubt it. Only by word of mouth, I suspect. Her death is still ruled a suicide. This doesn't change that."

"Is this a courtesy call or you got questions?" Massett asked, the gruff edge returning to his voice.

"Just wondering if you have anything to add? Any idea where she could have gotten them?"

I wondered if Griff was going to mention the large cash withdrawal Ashley made every month, but there was no reason the coach needed to know about that.

Massett shook his head. "I thought I knew my girls, but this…this I never would have guessed. Not in a million years. Not Ashley, especially not Ashley."

"Well, if you think of anything that might help we'd appreciate a call."

Coach Massett nodded. "Fair enough."

I feel sort of bad for the guy," I said as we walked back down the corridor. A blemish on his perfect girls."

"There's a lot of that going around," Griff said.

"A lot of what?"

"Perfect girls. Let's go see Mitzi."

We pulled into the brown ranch's driveway and parked in front of an empty garage.

"Guess Gary got his pickup running," I said.

"For the time being."

At the door, we were about to knock when it swung back about a foot. A woman in a gray sweat suit with a flowered apron tied at the waist looked out.

"Help you?"

She was early fifties with brittle hair that had been dyed red at some point, but was now a mix of gray and brown at the roots. Around her neck a gold chain held a crucifix and a medal of the Immaculate Conception.

"Hi," I reached my hand out. "I'm Britt Callahan. We're here to see Mitzi. We have a couple of questions about her teammate Ashley Lambert."

"The girl who jumped?"

"Yeah."

"You cops?"

"Private investigators working for the family. This is my partner Griff Cole."

Griff nodded. She looked at him squinting her eyes as she did. "I'm her mother, Loraine. Whadya want with Mitzi?"

"Like I said, we have a few questions about Ashley. We're trying to get some answers for the family."

She took a few steps back and opened the door wider. "Come in," she said.

Inside the small kitchen a fly buzzed above plates piled in the sink. New ones I hoped.

"Mitzi," her mother yelled with a force that almost matched Gary's. "Get down here." She motioned us toward the table. "Have a seat. Get you something?" she asked, pushing a Bible and a stack of papers off to one side of the checked tablecloth.

I sat down and glanced at the paraphernalia on the table, a tiny book of psalms, a Bible opened to the Lord's Prayer and scraps of paper with religious mantras.

"Don't mind that stuff," she said catching me looking. "I was just sayin' my morning devotionals."

I nodded and smiled. "That's nice."

"Who the hell else is gonna take care of me if He don't?" She raised her eyes to the ceiling and held them there for a moment as if awaiting His confirmation.

I looked at Griff. He grinned. I kicked him under the table.

"Now what?" Mitzi said walking into the kitchen.

It was nice to feel welcome in the little Christian home.

"We're here to ask if you knew about Ashley's drug use," Griff said.

Mitzi skipped a beat. Looked at her mother then back to us and shuffled her feet on the linoleum floor. "I told you. Ashley wasn't the type."

"The tox screen says differently."

Her eyebrows went up. "No shit? I wish I'd known. I'd have blown the fuckin' whistle on her."

"Mitzi," her mother fog horned. "Watch your language."

"Ma, I could have taken my rightful place, first through the ribbon."

"You never saw her talking to anyone on a regular basis?" Griff cut in. "No visitors in your dorm room that you didn't know?"

"Like I told you. The girl had no friends. I never saw her with anyone except for the team when she was at practice."

"Anybody hanging around practices?"

She shrugged. "Sometimes there was this dude she'd talk to."

"What did he look like?"

"I don't know. I never got close. It wasn't like she introduced him to anyone. He'd just be on the sideline somewhere and she'd go over and talk to him. I don't know if it was even always the same guy."

"What do you mean?"

"Sometimes he'd have on a cop uniform and sometimes he was riding a bicycle or sometimes he just looked regular. Could a been three different guys for all I know."

"You never saw his face?" I asked.

"He always had on a hat or a bike helmet and sunglasses."

"What was his build like?" I asked. Women usually notice a guy's physique.

She shrugged. "Medium, 5'10" or 11", I'm not sure. You think he was selling her drugs? I never saw her take anything from him. They'd just talk a minute and then he'd leave."

I looked at Griff. He raised his eyebrows.

"What?" Mitzi said. "You know who that is?"

Griff stood. "Thanks, Mitzi. You've been really helpful. We'll be in touch if we need anything else."

I followed Griff to the door and turned to thank Loraine, but she was already seated at the table paging through her bible, oblivious to us.

"Mike was Ashley's supplier," I said as we got into Griff's car.

"Makes perfect sense," Griff said. "How better to get back at someone than to mess with their kid?"

"His payback to Gwen for treating him like shit all those years was to screw up Ashley. What a bastard. And the large cash withdrawal..."

"Was either an exorbitant charge for the drugs he was supplying or he threatened to expose her drug use to the school and her parents which would have taken everyone down."

"She could have just told him she didn't want the drugs anymore."

"He had her either way. She needed the drugs to maintain her performance, which in turn maintained her family and kept Greg at home. If she stopped taking them she'd begin to lose meets, which meant losing Greg's interest, losing her family and Mike would expose her. She couldn't win. She was going to Johns Hopkins to major in Ethics and yet the way she was living couldn't have been more unethical. What else could she do but jump? At least by her way of thinking."

"So now what? Should we go give Greg and Gwen the news?"

"I don't know that we have enough evidence to point the finger. We have no definite proof of blackmail or drugs yet. It's all circumstantial at this point."

"We have Mitzi's description of a guy with Mike's build in a cop uniform or biking gear. We have his axe to grind with Gwen. We have the fact that he's living too large for someone with a cop's salary."

"Let me think about it. Anyway, I haven't got time right now. I'm meeting with Guy Hendricks at one o'clock."

"Who's that?"

"Our new case."

"The antique dealer?"

"Yeah. He and his accountant want to show me the discrepancies they've found over lunch then we're going to his warehouse. He's got some articles that aren't matching inventory and I need to get pictures. You want to come?"

"Not really. I mean it sounds interesting and I'll do whatever you need me to, but I thought I might hang around the house this afternoon so…"

"So you'll be close if Rhea needs you," Griff said completing my sentence.

I looked at him and nodded. "Okay?"

"More than okay. It's a good idea. I'll feel a lot better when that baby is born and the two of them are living miles away."

"What're we gonna do about Mike?"

"For now, nothing. He doesn't know what Mitzi's told us so there's no rush getting to Lambert's. It's going to have to wait until tomorrow. After I see Hendrick's I've got to go to the office for a while. I won't be late but go ahead and eat without me."

"Pick up Chinese on your way home and I'll open some wine. We'll have a late dinner."

"Even better," he said. "We've hardly spent a day together since buying the house."

"Tonight we'll make up for lost time."

Twenty-Five

It was five twenty-seven when Rhea called. I heard the phone and assumed it would be Griff telling me he was on his way, but when I slid my thumb across the screen to accept the call all I heard was breathing…hard, raspy breathing.

"Rhea?" I asked, my heart quickening.

"Britt, come quick."

At first I thought I'd dropped the call due to the silence that followed, but then I heard a crash, like a piece of furniture hitting the floor and then the scream. Rhea's scream…"Britt."

I dropped my phone on the counter and ran barefoot in a tee shirt and yoga pants for the front door, leaving it wide behind me. On the path through the trees, the overgrown lilac bushes devoid of their blooms grabbed at my arms and face. Roots that I'd barely known were there erupted from the dirt slowing my progress, stubbing my toes and bruising the soles of my feet. But it was Rhea's screaming my name that drove me forward as fast as I could move.

I flipped the metal u-bracket on the chain link fence and ran into the backyard, across the stone patio and up the stairs to the kitchen. Sliding back the glass door, I froze for a moment to take in the scene. Rhea was on her knees, bent over, her head grazing the floor, arms wrapped protectively around her bulging belly. Mike stood over her in uniform, his nightstick in hand. The kitchen was destroyed. A drawer of silverware upended on the floor. The pantry cabinet lay on its side, its contents, including the glass panels from its doors, strewn over the Mexican tile. That was the crash I'd heard on the phone. I started toward them.

Rhea looked up. "Britt," she said, whining like a kitten.

"What the hell do you want?" Mike said, his baton still hovering over Rhea's back. "Get the fuck out of my house."

I started toward him. "Put it down," I said hoping my voice wasn't as shaky as my knees.

"Screw you."

I kept moving forward.

"Britt, your feet," Rhea said, her voice stronger now.

I looked down at the bloody footprints I was leaving stepping on slivers of glass that littered the floor like chicken feed. It was everywhere, impossible to avoid. I kept walking.

"Get the fuck out." Mike's eyes bounced from Rhea to me, and back.

"We know about Ashley," I said hoping to shift his focus away from Rhea long enough for her move.

He looked at me. There was no missing the surprise in his eyes. "You don't know shit," he said. There was less strength in his voice.

"We know you were supplying her with drugs, performance enhancers to keep her winning and ultimately destroy her. The same way Gwen destroyed you by treating you like you were worthless and stealing your self-esteem. What better way to get back at her than to do the same thing to her daughter?"

He straightened up and lowered his arm. Still staring at me.

"Get up Rhea," I said. "Move away from him."

He glanced down at his wife as she began to rise. His arm twitched. He raised the baton.

"On top of the drugs, you were blackmailing her."

That caught his attention. He looked back at me.

"You were either charging her an exorbitant amount for the drugs or you were blackmailing her, promising to keep quiet about what lay at the root of her success as long as she kept paying you."

Rhea was now safely out of his reach, but he didn't seem to care. His eyes hadn't left my face.

"I never took money from Ashley. I didn't want their money. It was payment enough to watch Gwen dissolve when her golden child went down. I supplied the drugs, but that's all. In the beginning, everyone got what they wanted, success. But I knew it was only a matter of time before Ashley either physically or mentally gave out and I got what I wanted. Killing herself, killed her family. I had no beef with Ashley. She was a means to my end."

"Then how do you explain all this on a cop's salary?" I waved my hand indicating the million-dollar home they lived in.

"Guilt money from my father. It made him feel better after he abandoned my mother and me. I didn't give a fuck. I gladly took it when he offered. But I never took a dime from Ashley."

"We'll see about that. You'll have your day in court and you can explain it all then, but right now Rhea's coming with me." I moved past him trying to avoid the glass cutting like barnacles into the bottom of my feet.

"Like hell. She's not going anywhere."

"She needs to go to the hospital. Look at her."

Rhea's forehead was split, as was her top lip. Her left cheekbone looked like an over ripe peach, pulpy and wet.

Mike gazed at his wife's face. "You're not going anywhere like that." He turned back to me. "She stays here and you get the hell out. This is my house. I'll handle things."

"If you don't let me take her I'm going to the police. I'll tell them about Ashley and I'm gonna tell them what I saw when I walked in here, you beating the shit out of your wife. She might lie for you, but I sure as hell won't."

I moved toward Rhea. She was standing to Mike's right, leaning against the doorframe that led to the living room. From the look of her, I wasn't sure she could even make it to my house. I reached out my hand. Her eyes drifted from my face to what she saw behind me. They were wide with fear. I started to turn, but before I made it all the way around something hard hit the back of my head and the room went black.

"Britt, Britt…"

I could hear Rhea's voice but it was miles away. Swirling images in front of my face triggered a wave of nausea from my stomach to my throat. I closed my eyes, took a breath and tried again. "Rhea," I managed.

"I'm right here."

I felt a hand holding mine.

"Are you okay?"

Silence.

"Rhea," I said again. This time forcing my eyes open, fighting nausea back where it belonged.

Rhea was sitting beside me holding my hand. She was crying. "I'm okay," she said meeting my eyes. "But…"

I turned my head to survey the kitchen. Bad idea. A pain like a railroad spike drove itself through my head. "Where's Mike?" I managed.

She looked across the room and very carefully I followed her gaze. Mike was lying about six feet away, his head in a pool of blood. I stared at him for a few minutes trying to see the rise and fall of his body as he breathed. He didn't move.

"Is he?"

She nodded. "It was an accident, Britt. I didn't mean to kill him. After he hit you I went at him, beating his chest with my fists. He shoved me away. I fell. My hand landed on the baton where he'd dropped it. When he came at me, I swung it at his head. He fell and…and, I couldn't stop". Her voice dropped to a whisper. "I hit him again and again, his head, his chest and his head again. I couldn't stop."

I looked at her as she spoke, hearing the confession of a thousand battered women who once they'd murdered their abuser went into overdrive. Killing him repeatedly for every beating they ever took. I squeezed her hand.

"Help me," I said nodding toward the wall."

Rhea moved behind me and put her hands beneath my arms. I shoved my palms into the floor and scooted until I was leaning against the wall. On the back of my head I felt a lump the size of an apple and my hair was matted and wet against it.

"What do you need, Britt? What should I do?" She was on the verge of panic or shock. Either one could send her into labor. Not what we needed right now.

"Water," I said giving her something else to focus on. "Get me water, aspirin and…" I touched the back of my head. My hand came away smeared with blood. "Some gauze and tape."

Rhea disappeared down the hallway and I sat staring at Mike's lifeless body. He'd just come home from work. Had a bad day, ready to take it out on his wife, his pregnant wife. But she'd turned the tables first by calling me and then by delivering the deciding blows. Her rage had set her free. Blood saturated his hair, a matted mess stuck to his battered head. It had seeped onto the shoulders of his blue uniform shirt, turning it deep maroon.

"Here." Rhea knelt beside me. She dumped four aspirin into my hand, set the gauze and tape on my thigh and went to the sink for water stepping over Mike's body.

I took the glass and washed down the pills keeping my eyes on her face. "Are you alright? I mean, he's dead, are you.... "

"Sorry?" She shook her head keeping her eyes on mine. "Relieved and scared, but not sorry." She cradled her belly in the palm of her hand. "Are you going to call the police?"

"It's my duty as a PI and a public citizen to report a crime."

Rhea's eyes bore into me. "Britt, you know they'll arrest me. He's a cop. He's been beating me for years, but they'll never take my word over his. I'll go to prison for murdering my husband. "She ran her hand over her bulging stomach. "My baby..." her eyes filled with tears. "I can't lose this one too."

It was hard to think over the pounding in my head, not to mention my heart working triple time. "I saw what happened. I can vouch for you."

She shook her head. "No, you didn't see what happened. You were out cold. That's what you'll have to say when they put you under oath." Tears spilled onto her cheeks. "Britt, please, you can't. They'll never side with me over him."

I knew she was right. It was the ultimate travesty of justice. Women found guilty for killing their abuser. I looked around the kitchen as an idea started to form. I didn't have my cell phone so I couldn't call Griff and I wasn't sure I wanted to. Two things I love about him are his ethics and his honesty, but neither of those would be helpful right now. What I needed was a way to help Rhea hide what had happened.

"I'm not going to the police."

Her body visibly relaxed.

"We're going to make this look like an accident and we're never under any circumstance going to sway from our story. Can you do that?"

She caressed her stomach. "Yes. But what if we get caught?"

"We won't."

"Go get all of Mike's biking gear. Whatever he wears when he goes for a ride, right down to the socks, shoes, underwear, helmet, everything."

She got up nimbly for a woman in her ninth month of pregnancy. I listened for her to start up the stairs then I unwrapped two squares of gauze and ran a piece of tape around my head to hold them in place. I was sure the wound called for stitches, but that wasn't happening. I scooted over to Mike and began to undress him. By the time Rhea came back into the kitchen he was naked. She dropped his cycling attire onto the floor beside me.

Once he was dressed from his helmet to his shoes, even his wrist ID, we had to get him outside. No small feat for two women, one pregnant, one concussed. We dragged him to the door.

"Leave him here. I'm going to get my car."

I ran through the path. Every step sent a blade slicing through my head. Before going inside, I stopped beside the back deck and turned on the hose. I ran the icy water all over my feet, top and bottom, rinsing fresh and coagulated blood into the grass. I did the same with my hands, then slid open the back door, crossed the kitchen and grabbed my car keys, phone, sneakers and a baseball hat to cover my bandaged head.

Rhea was sitting at the kitchen counter when I returned.

"You okay?"

"Yes. You don't have to keep asking."

"Just checking. We need to get him outside to my car. Are you able to do that?"

"I think so."

"Do you have a tarp?"

"In the garage. I'll get it."

I watched her go down the stairs, gripping the railing. She wasn't okay, that much was plain on her face, but it wasn't regret. I took it as fear and maybe to some degree, shock over what had happened and what we were doing. She wasn't alone.

"Lay it out on the floor."

I wrapped a large bath towel around Mike's head to keep the blood from leaving a trail and we entombed him in the tarp.

"I'm going to slide him down the stairs," I told Rhea. "Stand at his feet so you can stop him if I lose my grip. I'll hold his head."

She nodded and stepped backwards onto the stone steps.

"Hold the rail," I said. "The last thing we need is for you to fall."

Together we slowly and carefully slid Mike's body down the stairs and over to my waiting car. I opened the rear door. Rhea started to lift his feet.

"Uh ah," I said. "No lifting. I can do this."

I took Mike's shoulders in a bear hug, wishing for the upper body strength I didn't have and slumped him into the cargo space in the back of the Rav. Lifting his feet next I worked him into the small area folding his legs behind him as though he were kneeling. I turned to Rhea who'd been standing off to the side watching.

"Now we need his bike," I said.

The fear or confusion or whatever that had been residing on her face left it as she understood my plan. "I'll get it." She disappeared toward the garage and in minutes came around the corner wheeling Mike's Colnago.

I took it from her, slipped the front wheel off and laid the bike and tire on top of his body then closed the back door.

"What's a common route for him to take? If he'd come home tonight and gone for a ride, where would he go?"

"I don't know exactly. He went out Route 9 a lot and picked up route 100. He stayed to the back roads."

I nodded. "While I'm gone you have to clean the kitchen, every speck. And I need his uniform including the baton in a trash bag."

We went back into the kitchen. There was glass and blood everywhere. Rhea handed me a green leaf bag from the cabinet above the refrigerator. And I stuffed all of Mike's police issue clothing and the baton into the bag.

"He's got plenty of uniforms, right? I mean they won't miss this."

"They're forever giving them new uniforms. I don't even know how many he's got."

I handed Rhea his shield and gun. "Put these wherever he keeps them when he gets home. And then get a bucket, fill it with detergent and bleach and clean this kitchen like you've never cleaned it before. Every inch."

She nodded.

"Get rid of the glass and the blood. We'll put the pantry cabinet in the garage when I get back. You can say you knocked it over and Mike put it in there until he had time to fix it. Then scrub the bucket too. Can you do that?"

She nodded again, staring at the floor.

"If it's too much, do what you can. I'll finish when I get back."

"I can do it. I have a compost pile way out back in the trees. I'll bury everything under that."

"That works," I said, impressed.

"What...what are you going to do with him?"

"He had a cycling accident or got run off the road or hit sand or whatever they want to believe when they find him. You'll have to call the police later to report him missing, but wait until I get back."

I left Rhea filling a bucket at the sink, the steam rising in her face as she stared out the window in front of her. I wanted to know what she was thinking, needed to know where her head was, but we didn't have time for emotions right now. That would come later.

I drove out Route 9 passing the Royal Oaks new development and noticed a gravel truck parked beside the hole that would very soon, be an in-ground pool. I pulled into the empty development and shut off the Rav's headlights. The dirt was raked smooth on the sides and bottom of the dug-out earth. The gravel in the truck was ready to be poured. I remembered the process from when our next-door neighbor's pool was installed. Amy and I had watched the installation when we were kids, with high hopes of being invited over for a swim. We never were. I turned back to the Rav glad I'd thought to bring a shovel.

I drove out Route 9 watching for the right spot. Occasionally I passed another car, but they were rare. I took a right onto a narrow dirt road with no street sign because it started with a steep hill and I was hoping it would have as steep a grade going down on the other side. The road narrowed at the crest and as hoped, careened down into an S-curve, steep enough to challenge even the most avid cyclist. There were no houses in sight, just pasture on the left and to my right, a plunging gravel drop. Made to order.

I pulled as tight as I could to the right side, which wasn't very far without teasing the edge of the cliff. But it was perfect for my needs as long as another car didn't pull up behind me.

I shut off the engine, dowsed the lights, put on the leather gloves I'd brought and opened the back door. Working as fast as my lack of strength allowed, I pulled Mike from the car and unrolled him from the tarp. I took the towel off his head trying not to look at his face, the face of my neighbor. The face of an abuser, I reminded myself. Before putting his bike helmet on him I beat it against the rocks near the car, smashing it against the granite with all my strength. When I'd finished, it was worn and scraped and cracked in a couple of places. I loosened the strap and put it on his head, shifting it to one side so that the clip was on his left ear and the helmet covered only the right side of his head. The less beaten side. Slipping my foot beneath him, I rolled him over the edge. It wasn't a huge drop, thirty feet, maybe a little more. His body somersaulted over the gravel and rocks, bounced off two separate boulders and came to rest close to the bottom.

Standing at the edge watching him roll, I thought for a minute I was going to be sick. But I couldn't let my mind grasp the reality of what my body was doing. I just had to get through it. I could feel it later.

I turned and walked back to the car. Removing the bike, I reattached the front wheel and with the shovel, beat on the bike frame and tires until everything was sufficiently bent, scraped and a few spokes were broken, then I rolled the bike over the edge. It took a couple of turns on its bent wheels, wobbling along like a child learning to ride then it toppled over and slid halfway down the ravine.

I surveyed my work, feeling like I was in the midst of an out of body experience. Covering up a crime was something I had people arrested for. The moon slipped from behind a cloud and glinted off the handlebars. I looked past them and down to where Mike lay. This was a man, a cop and a husband, soon to be a father. He was also a controlling, abusive asshole, a misogynist who had no ability to care for his pregnant wife let alone a helpless child. But he'd met this end not because he couldn't care for his family, but because he would physically harm them. "Not anymore, Mike," I whispered.

I added the tarp and towel to the trash bag then started the car and backed up until I was on the slope at the base of the S-curve. I hit the gas, braking hard as I neared the gravel along the edge causing the back end of the Rav to fishtail. My heart pounded in my ears. All I needed was to lose control and end up over the side with Mike. I pulled back onto the dirt road then stopped, checking my work in the rear-view mirror. The tire tracks came from the end of the S-curve toward the right side of the road. It was obvious where I'd hit the brake and skidded. Anyone looking at the scene would agree, the visual told the story. A vehicle either intentionally or unintentionally had run Mike off the road at the base of the hill, sending him over the edge. A hit and run. The only alternative was that he'd come off the s-curve too fast and lost control. I'd be content with either.

At Royal Oaks I doused my headlights and again took the shovel from the back as well as the leaf bag with Mike's gear. I left my flashlight in the car, no need to draw attention if anyone passed. The moon was on my side tonight. Its radiance was all the light I needed.

Whoever had left the ladder propped against the side of the hole would pay for that oversight in the morning when the crew returned, but his carelessness was my good luck. I tossed the bag into the would-be pool and climbed down the ladder holding the shovel with one hand. At the bottom, I dug a hole deep enough to cover the evidence and then added another foot. I threw in the leaf bag, covered it as quickly as I could and flattened the ground on top, hiding any sign of disturbance. Then crossed to the ladder, smoothing the ground with the back of the shovel to erase my footprints. At the top, I looked back. No trace of my having been there. Satisfied, I tossed the shovel in the cargo hold, slipped into the driver's seat and closed my eyes. Exhaustion took over and I felt the tears coming before they reached my eyes. I squeezed my lids shut. No time for that. I'd done what needed doing. As long as the truth never came out, Rhea and her child would have what so many other women and children in abusive relationships never get…a chance.

I opened my eyes and started the car. I'd call Rhea when I got home and tell her to call the police and report Mike missing. My cell rang just as I pulled onto the road.

"Hello?"

"Britt?" It was Rhea. "I'm in labor."

Twenty-Six

"I'm ten minutes away," I said to Rhea. "Call the station, ask them if anyone's seen Mike. Tell them he went for a bike ride and left his phone at home and that you're in labor."

Rhea didn't answer.

"Rhea…"

"Yeah, sorry, contraction."

"Can you hold on until I get there?"

"Yes." Her breathing was fast and shallow. "Where's…what did you do with…"

"Don't worry about that now. Call the station and tell them they need to find Mike. Tell them your neighbor's taking you to the hospital. Then leave a note on the kitchen counter for Mike."

"Okay."

I pushed END and called Griff.

"Hey, where are you? I just got home."

"Rhea's in labor. I'm taking her to the hospital." I left out that I'd been out of the house for the past three hours, making it sound like I already had Rhea in the car and we were on our way. Omission is a gray area.

"Where's Mike?"

"Out on his bike."

"In the dark?"

"He left a while ago, but forgot to take his phone."

"Can I do anything?"

"No, but I'll stay with her until he gets to the hospital. She left a note for him in the kitchen. He'll come when he gets home."

"Okay, do what you need to. Tell Rhea good luck. I hope it goes smoothly for her."

"I will…hey Griff?"

"Yeah?"

"I love you."

"I love you too, honey. See you soon."

I ended the call wondering if he'd still say that if he knew how I'd spent the last three hours. I'd done things tonight I'd never believed I was capable of. I'd saved a woman and child and if caught, I'd go to prison. Was I a hero or a criminal? Griff and I both had a passion for justice. It was the path we took that differed.

When I pulled into Rhea's driveway, she was doubled over at the bottom of the stairs, her hand clenched around the railing. A bag sat at her feet.

"Let's go," I said jumping out of the car and hurrying toward her.

"My hospital bag, Britt. Will you get it?"

I slung the bag over my shoulder and we moved slowly to the car. I opened the passenger door while she leaned on the hood and breathed through another contraction.

"How fast are they coming?"

"About four minutes apart."

"Shit, let's go."

She stared straight ahead out of the windshield, taking long, deep breaths and made no comment about my running yellow lights and weaving in and out of lanes on route 295.

"How's the kitchen? Do you need me to go back and finish?"

She shook her head exhaling a long slow breath. "Spotless. Except for the pantry cabinet. I couldn't move it. I'm sure all that scrubbing is what started this."

"Did you call the police station?"

"Yes. I told them that I was in labor and that you were taking me to the hospital. I said Mike was out on his bike without his phone and that if any of them heard from him to let him know."

I nodded. "Good."

"Britt, what did you do with…"

"He's in a gully on a dirt road off Route 100."

Rhea closed her eyes and shivered. I didn't know if her reaction was a result of the physical pain she was in or the image of Mike I'd just given her.

"I threw the bike in with him after I bent it up."

She looked at me and blinked back tears, but didn't speak.

I had to remember that this was a guy she'd loved at some point in her life. To me, he was nothing but a man undeserving of the title, but to her he'd meant something once upon a time."

"It looks like he either lost control and ran off the road or a hit and run," I said softening my tone.

"Would running off the road be enough to kill him?" She asked, wiping her nose with the back of her hand.

"The gulley is at the base of a long, steep S-curve. He'd have been going very fast coming down the hill. Yeah, I think a fall like that could kill someone."

The medical center came into view and the only sound for the rest of the drive was Rhea's slow and steady breathing. I pulled the Rav into a parking space in the emergency lot, had a moment of déjà vu, and ran through the electronic doors to grab a wheel chair from a collection lined up like grocery carts.

Rhea sank into the chair, I dropped her hospital bag on her lap and together we rolled into the ER. I have to admit I was glad that I was the one doing the pushing...of the chair that is.

The nurse at the desk took one look at Rhea and relieved me of my transport duties. "You stay here and register her," she said to me. "I'll take her up to delivery. This girl's ready to go."

I'm not sure how she knew just by looking at her face, but I wasn't going to argue. "I'll try to reach Mike," I told Rhea as the nurse wheeled her away.

I registered her as well as I could, without having all her personal information and handed the clipboard back to the receptionist.

"Third floor," she said.

At the nurses' station, I gave them Mike's name and phone number reiterating the 'out for a bike ride' story.

"Got a minute?" A nurse asked as I stepped inside Rhea's room.

"Sure." I followed her into the hallway.

What's up with her face?"

I looked at my feet and then back at the nurse. "You'll have to take that up with her husband when he gets here."

"Don't think we won't," she said. "It's not only my job. It's my mission when they come in like that."

I nodded, knowing it was a moot point and walked past her into Rhea's room. She was propped up against starched white sheets. Her hair fanned out wildly around her head and her face was wet with sweat. A doctor had checked the baby's progress on making its exit, or entrance, depending on your perspective.

"Won't be long," she smiled as she passed me at the doorway. "Did you reach her husband?"

"Not yet. I'll keep trying."

She nodded and disappeared into the next room.

"Hey," I said standing beside the bed and taking Rhea's hand.

She gave me a squeeze in acknowledgement but kept focused on the nurse on the other side of the bed who was helping her regulate her breathing.

All of a sudden, she let out a yell and squeezed my fingers until I thought they might break. And just as I was about to match her with a screech of my own, she relaxed her grip.

"Jeez," I said.

The nurse shot me a dirty look. "Are you her support person?"

"Ah, I guess so."

"Then act like one."

I wanted to say that I'd done more to support Rhea and her baby than she could imagine, but I mumbled, "Sorry," instead, and pulled the green vinyl chair up to the bedside. Never letting go of Rhea's hand.

After another half hour of contractions, the doctor returned confirming it was time to push. They repositioned Rhea into a sitting posture and bent her legs at the knees. The doctor draped a sheet over her legs and took a seat front and center.

"Let's bring this baby into the world," she said with a smile.

Rhea groaned and the end game began.

I stayed at the head of the bed, wiping Rhea's face with a cool cloth as gently as I could, given her bruised and swollen skin. I thought about Griff and wondered if we'd ever be in a similar situation as the one I was in with Rhea now. He was ready to take our relationship to the next level. For me, moving into the house together was enough, but a year from now? Six months? Never say never.

"Your baby's crowning," the doctor said. "It won't be long. A few more good pushes."

She was right. On the fourth push Rhea's daughter emerged, coming from the warmth and safety of the womb into a world of no guarantees. The doctor laid the tiny, slippery, waxy-coated child on her mother's stomach. Rhea gathered her daughter into her arms and nestled the newborn's head against her neck, covering the baby's cheek with kisses and tears. Watching this moment between mother and child I thought for the first time…maybe. I kissed Rhea on the top of her head and walked into the hallway letting the nurses do their thing and giving Rhea time with her daughter without an audience.

Griff answered his phone on the first ring.

"It's a girl," I said.

"That's great. How's Rhea?"

"She's good. It was amazing to watch."

"Did Mike get there?"

My stomach clenched. "No, I still haven't been able to reach him. Do you want to run next door? See if his bike's there?"

"Sure. I'll call you back."

I hit the END button feeling a little guilty for sending Griff on what I knew to be a fruitless errand, but I had to play this to a tee. What came next sent my heart knocking against my ribs. I took a breath and called the police station. After explaining who I was and where I was, I told the desk clerk that Mike still hadn't been located.

"Hey, Cheevers." I heard the cop yell just before he put me on hold.

When he got back on the line he told me he had a couple officers who would take a ride around Mike's cycling routes in case he was out there with a flat tire or something.

Or something, I thought. I thanked the cop and gave him my number.

My hands were shaking when I dropped the phone back into my pocket. It was only a matter of time now before they found him and came to tell Rhea that Mike was dead. I looked down at my hands and realized for the first time what I must look like to the nurses. I'd picked up Rhea directly after staging Mike in the ditch and then climbing into the yet-to-be swimming pool and burying his gear. My fingernails were filthy and the creases in my palms were filled with grime. My shoes and yoga pants were covered with dust. If the police came and saw me like this, it may raise some suspicion. I took the elevator to the gift shop.

Hospital gift shops tend to carry a little of everything. I took a pair of black sweat pants, a matching zippered top and a Sea Dogs baseball hat to the register and handed the woman behind the counter my credit card. In the nearest bathroom, I stripped off my filthy tee shirt and pants, washed my face, wiped down my shoes with a wet paper towel and put on my new outfit, depositing everything inside the trashcan. I hadn't thought about needing to get rid of my clothes, but when I tossed them into the barrel I realized that traces of my evening endeavor were undoubtedly written all over them. Getting rid of the evidence should have been a priority. Every criminal makes a mistake. I hoped I'd just rectified mine.

When I got back to Rhea's room no one seemed to notice my change in attire. Rhea was propped up against fresh pillows holding her now bathed and swaddled daughter and smiling a smile that only a new mother can project.

"Britt," she said looking up, her smile fading slightly.

"She's perfect."

"I'm going to name her Delia, after my mother."

I laid my palm lightly against the baby's head. "That's a beautiful name."

"Has anyone…"

I shook my head. "Griff's going over to your house to see if Mike's there. And I called the station. They said a couple of officers would drive around the area where he rides in case he got a flat tire."

She nodded, her eyes holding mine. But it wasn't fear I saw in them anymore. It was more like a wariness or caution. She had someone other than herself to protect now and her determination showed.

I wished I could change the way it had all played out. I wished she could feel nothing but joy in this moment. But I'd done all I could to ensure that her future would be better than her past. It was what happened now that I couldn't control.

Scar Tissue

Griff called and told me Mike's bike had not been at the house and asked if I wanted him to come to the hospital. I told him no and said that I'd be home as soon as Mike arrived. An hour later two cops walked into the room. Their eyes were on Rhea and their faces told us what they were about to say before they opened their mouths.

"Hi, Jim," Rhea said with a smile. I could have kissed her. In no way did she look fearful or expectant. She shifted Delia in her arms. "Want to take a peek?"

The cop turned his hat in his hands. "Rhea," he said. "We found Mike."

She raised her eyebrows expectantly. "Is he coming? He has a daughter to meet."

In all the time I'd known Rhea, she'd never been so smooth, so confident, so committed to a cause.

"Rhea," the cop said. "Mike had an accident. We're not sure what happened, yet."

Rhea held his eyes, waiting.

"He went off the side of the road over an embankment. Or, it could have been a hit and run. We don't know, but believe me we'll find out."

"Where is he? Is he hurt?"

"Rhea," the cop kept twisting his hat. "I'm so sorry...the fall killed him."

She kept staring at him as though she didn't understand what he'd said. The room was silent. Even the nurse stopped bustling around, her eyes shifting from Rhea back to the cop.

"Do you want me to hold her for a minute?" I asked stepping up to the bedside and reaching for the baby.

Rhea shook her head. "No, no...I need..." Her voice trailed off and she buried her head into Delia's pink blanket and began to cry.

The cop shifted from one foot to the other, looking miserable.

"C'mon." I motioned them into the hallway. "What happened?" I asked once we were out of earshot from the room.

"We found him off Route 100. He'd gone off the side. Looked like he'd lost control and skidded over the edge or he could have been run off the road."

"Can you find out who did this?"

The cop shrugged. "Won't be easy. The road's a short cut from 100 over to Route 9. Not a lot of people use it 'cause it's dirt and full of potholes, but there are enough tire tracks that there's no way of knowing which ones sent Mike over the edge, or even if that's what happened. It could have been his error. It'll be tough to get an answer on this. I didn't want to tell his wife that, though."

I nodded. "I don't blame you. Where is he now?"

"Downstairs, in the morgue."

"Shit."

"Yeah," the cop said. "What happened to her face?"

At this point it didn't much matter what I said. I shrugged. "That's another story. I'm her neighbor. I'll stay with her. Does she need to do anything as far as you're concerned?"

The cop shook his head. "No. Tell her we'll let her know if we find anything. Oh, and the chief will be in touch to make funeral arrangements. He'll be buried with full honors."

I watched them go to the elevator and felt like a thousand pounds had just dropped off my shoulders. They'd read the scene the way I'd hoped. Now if it just stayed that way Rhea and I would be free and clear, at least where the law was concerned.

Twenty-Seven

I left Rhea and Delia snuggled tight against each other, sleeping. Best place for both of them. I hoped once home, I could do the same, but doubted my adrenalin surge was going to abate anytime soon. Rhea had left the pantry cabinet on the floor. One last job before I could leave this day behind.

I flipped on the lights and stepped into Mike and Rhea's kitchen. Standing still, I surveyed Rhea's clean up. She was right. The room looked spotless. No one would suspect that only a few hours earlier this had been the scene of a beating and then a murder. It was hard to wrap my head around everything that had taken place. And right now, I didn't have time to try. I wanted this over with. I wanted to get home to Griff.

I slid the heavy pantry cabinet across the floor over to the back door then scraped it down the stone steps and dragged it into the garage. Rhea could say it was being refinished if anyone asked, but I doubted they would. I felt confident that what I'd done tonight, and our story, would keep us in the clear.

The house was dark when I pulled into the driveway, but the branches hanging over the roof were lit with a golden hue coming from the skylights. Griff was waiting up.

I closed the front door behind me and let my bag fall to the tiled entryway. Suddenly weary, I knew my night was far from over. Griff would want to know everything that had happened.

Everything? I asked myself as I headed for the kitchen.

Opening our makeshift liquor cabinet, I perused our stash and reached for the Cinnamon Whiskey. I'm not a whiskey drinker. I rarely indulge in anything stronger than wine, but tonight called for something heftier than grapes.

"I'll get the glasses," Griff said coming up behind me, kissing my neck and taking a couple of rocks glasses from the cupboard.

"Must have been a rough labor if you're hitting the hard stuff. Mike show up?"

I turned toward him leaning my hip against the counter and watched him pour. I love Griff. There's no one I'm closer to except maybe Amy. And there's nothing he doesn't know about me, but right now, at this moment, he doesn't know that I've covered up a crime…a murder. So, should he know? Will it make our relationship stronger? Or, will it threaten his belief that someday I should be the mother of his child? After all, if I could do this, what else might I be capable of?

I took the glass he offered and swallowed half then refilled it without speaking.

"Whoa, that bad?" He capped the bottled and replaced it on the shelf, slung his arm around my shoulder and steered me toward the stairway. "Tell me all about it."

"Mike's dead," I said planting my foot on the first step.

"What?" Griff stopped.

"Biking accident. He went off the road out near Route 100. Cop said it could have been a hit and run, but the chances of finding the driver are pretty slim."

"A biking accident? On the day his baby is born? That's awful. How's Rhea?"

"Torn, I think. I mean she was a little teary. She must have loved him at some point. She married him. Truthfully? I think she's feeling more relief than grief."

I went into the bathroom and took off my hat, grateful that it had hidden my bandaged head from Griff. I wasn't sure yet how much I was going to say. Under the spray of the shower, I watched rivulets of dirt and blood run off my skin. When the water ran clear I toweled off, took another handful of ibuprofen and slipped into bed beside him.

We lay on our backs staring at the ceiling, shoulders and thighs touching. I kept wondering if I should come clean, tell him the whole grisly story, but the words wouldn't come. So, I said nothing, just sipped my whiskey until my head felt comfortably fuzzy and my eyes began to close. I felt Griff take the glass from my hand, heard the click of the bedside lamp being turned off and drifted into darkness.

It was the bacon that woke me. But my culinary pleasure was short lived when the memory of last night crushed me like a wave. Mike was dead by Rhea's hand and buried by mine. I made it to the bathroom in time to hang my head over the toilet and vomit all of last night's images into the basin. Beating the bicycle with the shovel, the tires, his helmet then affixing it to his already lifeless head. Sending him over the edge with a flip of my toe. It had all been so easy, too easy. What kind of person was I that I could, without hesitation, dispose of another human being? An asshole yes, but still a person.

"Hungry?" Griff called up the stairs.

I leaned my head out the bathroom door grasping the knob to hold myself up. "Be right down." I cupped my hands under the faucet and splashed cold water into my face. When I stood vertigo took over. I grabbed the sink to steady myself. When my feet felt stable, I lifted a towel from the rack and dropped my head into it, spinning in the darkness. After a double dose of ibuprofen, I looked in the mirror. My face looked the same. But nothing about me felt the same. I was capable of things I'd never thought possible. And none I was proud of.

"You look terrible," Griff said.

"Thanks."

"Sorry, I don't mean terrible, I guess just tired."

"It was a rough night."

"Maybe watching Rhea give birth took more out of you than you were prepared for." He set a plate in front of me and kissed my head.

I winced.

"You okay?"

"I fell helping Rhea out her kitchen door. Banged my head on the stone steps. It's just a lump. It'll heal."

"Jesus, Britt. Why didn't you say something when you got home last night? Want some ice?"

I waved him away. "I'm fine," I lied.

He poured our coffee and took a seat on the stool beside me. "I thought we should pay a visit to Greg and Gwen this morning and wrap this whole thing up."

"I thought you wanted more evidence?"

"I've come around to your way of thinking. We give the Lamberts our rendition of what happened and they can do with it whatever they want."

Griff had the partial story. Mike had hooked Ashley on PEs to get back at his half-sister, but he hadn't deliberately sent Ashley off the edge. Like he'd said, she was just a means to his end. He'd wanted Gwen to pay for the pain she'd caused him. And as far as Mike's money, that had come from the man at the helm of it all, his father. Should I clear it up for Griff? Bring to light the gray areas? I sipped my coffee and debated. If I told him Mike had denied the blackmailing part of our theory then I'd also have to tell him about the conversation in the kitchen and that he'd been beating up Rhea and she'd called me to come over. It would lead to the whole story. I closed my eyes. It felt too complicated. I wasn't ready. My head was pounding.

"If her drug use came out," Griff went on, "it would have destroyed the family. She knew that. Stepping off an eighteen-story building seemed like a better option than risking the truth."

"Truth can be a scary thing."

"It shouldn't be. Not when it comes to family."

"Depends on the family and their stability."

"Stable or not every family has a history. And it shows up sooner or later."

We drove down Route 9, taking the back roads into Portland. I wasn't ready to relive the haunts of last night. I bent my head and fiddled with the zipper on my boot so I didn't have to look at the scenery.

"Hey they're finally pouring it," Griff said. "Guess they figure it'll be a selling point once the condos go on the market."

I looked up. We were passing Royal Oaks. The top half of the cement mixer was tilted on its bed. Gray cement oozed like frosting through a chute, flowing into the hole that would soon be a swimming pool and burying forever Mike McKenzie's blood-soaked police uniform. I swallowed bile burning my throat.

"You okay? You look pale," Griff said.

Before another lie slipped through my teeth his phone rang.

"Shit," he said. "We'll be there."

I looked at him, waiting.

"That was Carole. She was going through Ashley's things and found a journal. She said we need to read it, now."

Carole lived in South Portland, just a couple miles shy of her sister and the wealth of Cape Elizabeth. Her home was on a family-friendly dead-end street, a modest two-story, ivy-covered bungalow that exuded warmth, unlike her sister's million-dollar dwelling.

We parked at the curb and before reaching the porch Carole opened the door, a red leather book in her hand. It was obvious she'd been crying. She pushed the book into Griff's chest. "Read this," she said. "That poor child."

We stepped into the living room. Griff sank into an overstuffed couch and I sat on the arm of it hunched over his shoulder. The first entry was dated a year ago, at the start of the school year and made reference that *"things"* were continuing with *him* as they had been, but the entries didn't explain what *"things"* were or, who *"him"* referred to. As we continued to read, it became clear that the male she mentioned only by pronoun was supplying her with drugs and had been for quite some time. She was distraught, becoming increasingly self-loathing as we turned the pages. She could not continue, could not ethically claim her seat at Johns Hopkins, she was worthless. Her self-deprecation increased with every entry. It became almost too painful to read as we accompanied this young woman on the thought process that led her to end her life.

"Wait a minute," Griff said. "Read this."

I followed his finger down the page.

"They're going to notice the missing money. I've begged her to stop. I've given her enough. I've offered to throw races and let her win. But "M" promises to expose me if I stop paying her. I don't know what to do. They're going to look at my account sooner or later. I can't let them know what I've done. It will destroy them."

"M?" I looked at Griff. "Mitzi was blackmailing Ashley?"

"It makes sense," he said. "She saw Mike at the field. She probably knew exactly what was going on."

"So why didn't she go to the coach?"

"Because money was more tempting than being first across the finish line."

"Does Gwen know about this?" I asked Carole.

"I called her and read it to her just before I called you."

"Was she going to call the police?"

"She said she wanted to talk with you first."

Griff nodded. "We'll head over to the house, but I want to see Mitzi first. Hear it from the horse's mouth."

Back in the car Griff stepped hard on the accelerator. It was at least a half hour drive from South Portland to Falmouth. "Let's hope we get there before Greg," Griff said.

"You think he'll go to Mitzi's?"

"I hope not, but I'd feel better if Carole hadn't called them. Mitzi's at least in part responsible for their daughter's suicide. Wouldn't you want to pay her a visit if it was your kid?"

I thought about Rhea loving Jonathan so much that she'd given him up rather than have him grow up in a violent home. And I remembered Griff's grief when he'd pulled Allie from the bowels of the basement where she'd been left by a serial killer. "I guess any parent would."

"Damn right," Griff said. "We need to get there first."

"You think he'll do something?"

"Grief, anger, blame…they all top rational thinking."

I looked out the window and saw Mike's mottled, swollen face, my own hands securing the helmet around his bloody, beaten head and nodded in agreement.

Twenty-Eight

When we turned down Western Ave. it was quiet. No sign of Greg's navy-blue BMW outside of Mitzi's house. I breathed a sigh of relief. That's all we needed was Greg confronting Mitzi before we could talk to her.

Griff pulled into the driveway and cut the engine. "Let's go in and see if Mitzi will talk. I'm sure Greg and Gwen will call the police, if they haven't already, and once she realizes she's getting arrested I doubt she'll be talkative. We need a confession first."

We walked toward the door, past the statue of the Virgin Mary waist deep in weeds. The garage door was closed indicating that Gary's beater was still running. Griff knocked on the weather stained, wooden door.

"Somebody at the door."

It was Gary's voice.

"I'm busy. You get it," Loraine said.

I glanced at Griff.

"Couple of socialites." He knocked again.

"Mitzi," Loraine yelled. "Get the door."

After some shuffling the door swung open. Mitzi registered surprise at the sight of us standing on her steps. "What do you want?" she asked. "I already told you everything I know."

"From what we just read in Ashley's journal, I'd say not quite everything. Do you want to invite us in or talk about it out here?" Griff asked.

Mitzi glanced over her shoulder at her parents then grabbed a jacket off the coat rack beside the door and stepped outside.

"What did you read in her journal?"

"That you were blackmailing her. $8000 a month, I think it was? Correct me if I'm wrong."

Mitzi didn't answer. She dug the toe of her Nikes into the dusty July ground.

"That guy that was coming to the track was supplying her with performance enhancers," I said. "But you'd already figured that out, hadn't you?"

Mitzi nodded. "Last year," she said.

I was surprised that she hadn't tried to deny the accusation, but she was still a kid, twenty-one at the most and out of her league when it came to extortion. Her shoulders drooped and she sighed. She almost seemed relieved.

"We don't have much." She nodded toward the brown ranch. "My parents do the best they can. I'm on scholarship. That rich bitch had everything. At the top of her class and the number one women's track athlete. When they first put us together I was a sophomore, she was a junior. I looked up to her, but by the end of the second term I resented the hell out of her. I started seeing that guy at practices. I thought it was a boyfriend at first, but when I asked she said he was just a friend."

"Didn't the coach ask who he was?"

"No, he probably didn't notice him. Most of the time he came to our dorm room. Once I walked in on them counting out pills. Another time, Ashley had a rubber tourniquet around her arm. After he left she begged me not to tell anyone. She said she'd do anything I wanted. At first, I told her to forget it. I wouldn't tell. But then I got the idea that maybe she should pay me not to tell. I know it was stupid, but she had plenty of money." She shuffled her feet against the patchy, overgrown front lawn. "Look at our house." She nodded again toward the brown ranch. "We struggle. My dad needs a new truck. My mom hasn't bought herself anything in years. I saw a way to help. I knew the amount of money I was asking for wouldn't make a dent in Ashley's life. I told her she had to pay me or I'd go to the coach and the dean of students and turn her in. I never meant for her to freak out over it. I was gonna let it drop once she graduated. She'd be gone. I'd be number one on the track and have money to help my family. It all seemed pretty harmless until she killed herself."

I glanced at Griff and shook my head. This young woman's life was about to be ruined. She'd be pulled out of college just before her senior year, pulled off the track at the peak of her athletic career and dropped into prison. All for less than $100,000. Mitzi had tried to help her family and give herself a step up. Not that what she did was right, but it was understandable.

At first the crack didn't register as a gunshot. I heard it but couldn't place it so out of context. But when I saw the hole in Mitzi's forehead I knew exactly what the sound had been. She stared into my face and I watched her eyes go from shock to understanding. Her knees crumpled and before her head hit the ground, she was dead.

Griff was running toward the shooter.

I knelt beside Mitzi and lifted her head onto my lap. The screen door banged.

"Mitzi," Loraine screeched.

Feet pounded the ground behind me and a hand gripped my shoulder. Loraine dropped onto the grass and tore Mitzi from my grasp.

"Give her here," she said.

But I was unable to tear my eyes from Griff, his arms wrapped around Gwen. The gun still dangling from her hand.

"You son of a bitch," Gwen yelled, straining against Griff's straightjacket grip. "You nasty little whore. You killed my daughter."

Out of nowhere Gary came running. He passed Loraine and I kneeling on the ground and ran straight toward Gwen. He planted his fist in her face. Blood sprayed from her nose onto his chest and down Griff's arm. The gun fell from her grasp and landed at her feet. Gary drew his arm back ready to swing again. Griff twisted around and the blow caught him between the shoulder blades knocking the wind out of him. He and Gwen hit the ground.

From across the street someone came running toward the house.

"Gary," a man yelled, coming into the yard. He headed straight to where Gary was kneeling alongside Griff and Gwen pulling at Griff's shoulders trying to untangle them, wanting another clear shot.

"Gary, buddy." The guy shook the big man's shoulders. "Gary, stop." He tried to turn Gary's face toward him and away from Gwen.

"She shot Mitzi," Gary said in a midst of snot and tears, wiping his face with the back of his forearm.

"The police are coming. Let them sort it out, man, not you. You're gonna get in trouble."

Gary sat back on his heels, dazed. He looked at his neighbor then across the yard. His eyes searching out his wife. On his hands and knees, he crawled over the burnt grass of his front lawn to his dead daughter. Laying his head in his wife's lap beside his daughter's he collapsed.

My heart pounded in my ears, pushing Gary's sobs and Loraine's wails to background noise. Mitzi lay in her mother's lap, dead by another mother's hands. Loraine and Gwen were worlds apart, but strip away the money and they were one in the same. Mothers destroyed by their daughters' best intentions.

Two police cars and an ambulance pulled into the driveway as I was getting up and going to where Griff stood. Gwen still in his arms for protection or consolation. But Gary was no longer a threat, sobbing on the ground beside his daughter's body. EMT's attended to Mitzi while two uniforms handcuffed Gwen. Reading her rights, they escorted her to the back of one of the cruisers. After taking our statements along with the statement of Gary's neighbor, we watched the convoy leave followed by Gary and Loraine in the rusty, blue F-150.

The quiet Falmouth neighborhood returned to the way it had been when we'd arrived not more than thirty-minutes ago. Amazing how life can change in half an hour.

Twenty-Nine

A month had passed since the debacle at Mitzi's house and we were both beginning to feel normal again. Well, Griff was anyway. I was still debating whether or not to come clean to him about Mike's death. I knew at some point in my life I would tell him. I just wasn't sure when that time would come and how much I'd lose when it did.

I was sitting on the front porch in one of the Adirondack chairs enjoying the sun on my face and a Honey Berry on my lips when my cell rang.

"Britt, I closed on the sale of the house this morning," Rhea said. There's a mover coming this weekend. Delia and I are leaving tomorrow."

I knew she had to go, but I was sorry to lose her. We'd been through a crazy amount of shit together for a friendship that had just started.

"We're heading to Bar Harbor this morning. We'll be gone for the weekend," I told her as Griff came out of the house with our suitcases.

"Can you come by? Just for a minute, before you go."

"I'll be right over."

Griff looked at me and raised his eyebrows? "Rhea?"

"She closed on the house. She'll be gone by the time we get home."

He nodded toward the path. "Go ahead."

I jogged through the path wondering how long it would take before it became overgrown. Until vines, branches and roots erased any trace of the footsteps it had fostered and the hands that had built it.

Rhea was at the gate when I emerged from the woods and swung it wide. A bittersweet smile played on her lips. "Britt," she said wrapping me into a hug.

Her post-baby body was soft against me.

"I'm really going to miss you," I said. "I don't have huge numbers in the friend department."

She laughed. "Their loss. I've never known anyone quite like you."

We looked at each other for a brief moment. Each of us acknowledging the depths our friendship had taken us to.

"Where will you go?" I asked.

"I'm thinking Paris, maybe. I've never been out of the states."

I remembered her telling me that Jonathan had been adopted by a European family. Maybe she knew more about his whereabouts than she'd let on. I didn't ask. "I'm happy for you, Rhea."

I really was happy for her. Happy that Mike was dead and that she and Delia could go on and have a life together where she wouldn't always be looking over her shoulder.

"Thank you, Britt." Her voice broke and she hugged me again. "No one has ever gone to the lengths you did for me. Will you be alright?"

"I'll be fine."

"Did you tell Griff?"

I shook my head. "Maybe someday."

"I know what you risked. And what you still risk."

"It was worth it." I leaned in and gave her a final hug then stepped back still holding her hand and wiping the tears off my cheeks with the other. "Good luck, Rhea. Please stay in touch."

"I will. You can count on it."

I went out the gate and back down the path toward home feeling the loss in the pit of my stomach. I stopped mid path, took a pack of Honey Berries from my back pocket and lit up. Rhea wondered if I'd tell Griff. So did I. It was too big a secret to keep from him forever. I already felt differently about myself. He'd notice the change. My hands had taken on a slight tremor, a manifestation of my inner world. I could not fall asleep at night without replaying the image of myself bashing Mike's helmet against the rocks, battering his bicycle with the shovel and kicking his beaten body into the ravine. Every time I passed the pool I thought of the evidence buried beneath it. I'd saved a life. Two lives. For that, I wasn't sorry. But, who was I? What was I? I took another drag from the cigar and without an answer emerged from the path into our driveway. Griff was stretched out in one of the Adirondacks as I approached. The suitcases beside him.

"No smoking in the car," he said, standing.

"That's why I'm having it now."

"Rhea doing okay?"

"She's good. They'll be fine."

"I'll put the bags in. You ready?"

I stamped out my cigar. "Yeah, just let me make a quick run through the house to be sure."

I checked the windows and their locks and looked in the bathroom to see that I'd packed the essentials, make-up, toothbrush and hairdryer. My cell phone was in my bag with a charger. I grabbed a bottle of wine from the rack on my way through the kitchen to have when we got to the hotel.

The back of the Rav was open and Griff was leaning against the door when I stepped outside. Our suitcases stood in the driveway in front of him. It was clear from his face something was wrong. And then I saw it. Mike's ID band in Griff's hand. Rhea had said that he wore it whenever he went for a ride, so we'd made sure he had it on when I loaded him into the back of my car.

"Found this in the underneath stowaway. How'd it get into your car?" He twirled the band around his fingers.

I didn't answer. I knew someday this moment would come. I just didn't think it would come so soon. I thought I'd be the one to bring it up and have time to prep.

"Have a seat," I said and motioned to the back bumper on the Rav. I sat beside him and lit another Honey Berry. "The night Delia was born Mike didn't go for a ride on his bike. He went for a ride in the back of my car. It must have fallen through the crack in the cargo space floor."

Griff looked at me. "I'm not following."

I started at the beginning with Rhea's phone call telling me to come quick. I told him how I'd arrived at McKenzie's house and seen it torn apart, Mike volatile, telling me to get out and then admitting to giving Ashley drugs, but not to blackmailing her.

"Why didn't you tell me any of this?"

I held up my hand. "Let me finish. Anyway, we'd pretty much already figured out that he was Ashley's supplier at that point. We just didn't know who was blackmailing her."

I went on and told him how Mike had hit me and I'd been knocked out. When I woke up Mike was dead. Rhea had killed him. Unintentionally at first, but when it felt so good she'd kept at it.

Griff shook his head. "Jesus."

"This is the part I'm not real proud of and the part you might rather not know 'cause if you do, you might feel like you need to do something about it."

"Like, tell the truth and turn you in?"

I nodded. "Yeah, 'cause that's the kind of guy you are. It'll torment you trying to decide between me and what's right."

Griff drew his mouth in a line and stared at the ground. "You really think that? You really believe I'd turn you in?"

"You haven't heard the whole story."

"Go on."

I told him every detail and my stomach twisted and churned as I explained adjusting the strap on Mike's helmet and pushing his body off the edge. I told him my relief when I saw the cement being poured into what was now a glistening blue pool at Royal Oaks, hiding forever any evidence of Mike's bloody uniform. And then I looked at him, my heart bruising my rib cage.

"You should have called me."

"You're a by the books kind of guy. You're honest to a fault. If I'd pulled you into it, it would have gone against everything you stand for and everything I love about you. I didn't want to get you dirty."

"But now I know. Makes me dirty by association."

I looked at him. "Unless you do something about it."

He was quiet, staring at his hands folded together, one thumb rubbing the knuckle of the other. "Let's go." He stood, tucked the ID bracelet into the front pocket of his jeans, got into the driver's side of the Rav and turned the key. The engine responded. We turned onto the main road in silence.

After about an hour of my stomach doing backbends, I looked at him. "You angry?"

He shook his head, but didn't speak.

I watched the pine trees sweep past and tried to calm my heart. Griff would never turn me in, but was he regretting the house and the deeper commitment between us that buying it symbolized?

"I don't know how I feel, Britt," he said. "I'm disappointed that you felt you couldn't call me for help, but I'm touched that you hold me in such high regard. Yeah, I try to be an honest person, but maybe it's to a fault. It's not worth it if it means when you're in trouble you can't come to me."

He reached over and took my hand and my stomach unclenched a little.

"I'm sorry you had to go through all that alone. It must have been awful."

Tears burned my eyes and I turned again to look at the trees.

"I'm proud of you for being so brave, for doing what you had to for Rhea's sake. I'd like to think I'd have done the same had I been in your position. I don't know. Maybe you're right. Maybe I would have called the police. Let the justice system take over."

"That was my fear," I said. "That justice would never be done if I gave it a chance."

We drove on in silence. I kept weighing the pros and cons of honesty and assumed Griff was doing the same. A gas station appeared ahead and he flipped the blinker on. We pulled up alongside the pumps. Griff got out. Reaching into his pocket he took out Mike's ID bracelet, turned it over a few times in his hand then tossed it into the trash receptacle.

When we pulled back onto the road, he reached over and entwined his fingers through mine. "We're a team. Next time you're in trouble, call me."

"I don't want to change who you are."

"You won't. But relationships are about having each other's backs. And you need to know I have yours. No matter what."

"Even if I get you dirty?"

He smiled, looking pensive. "A little dirt never hurt anyone."

THE END

Patricia Hale

Acknowledgements

A huge thanks to the incredible team at Intrigue Publishing, Austin Camacho, Denise Camacho and Susan McBride. You have been my support throughout this journey. I am indebted. A heartfelt thank-you to my editor, Melanie Rigney, for your enthusiasm, guidance and for cleaning up after me. My deepest gratitude to my readers, Eric Poor and Tina Perry Buckley for your time and for seeing the things I overlooked. As always, my love and thanks to my family, from my mother to my grandchildren and everyone in between for all your encouragement and faith. And lastly, but mostly, to Mike, Enya and Muddy, who despite all the missed walks and late dinners, keep wagging their tails.

AUTHOR BIO

Patricia Hale received her MFA degree from Goddard College. Her essays have appeared in literary magazines and the anthology, My Heart's First Steps. Her debut novel, *In the Shadow of Revenge*, was published in 2013. *Scar Tissue* is the third book in her PI series featuring the team of Griff Cole and Britt Callahan. Patricia is a member of Sister's in Crime, Mystery Writers of America, NH Writer's Project and Maine Writer's and Publisher's Alliance. She lives in New Hampshire with her husband and two dogs.